CHAPTER 1

17 DECEMBER

Zoey stood at the entrance of her little market stall and watched the sky as tiny snowflakes swirled in the air. It had been trying to snow for the last few days without any real success, almost as if the heavy grey clouds above them just couldn't be bothered to produce copious amounts of the white stuff and were only making a token effort to show willing. If this were an office job, these clouds would be the ones carrying a big sheaf of paper to look busy while really putting in minimal effort. By the time the snow touched the floor it had almost melted away. What she wouldn't give for a thick blanket of the stuff like you saw in those old-fashioned Victorian-themed Christmas cards with children carolling around the big tree. She sighed.

Still, there was just over a week left until Christmas Day so there was time for the weather to get its act together and fully commit to a white Christmas. She loved Christmas – the decorations, the smells, the food, the cheesy movies – but it wasn't quite the same without an abundance of snow.

1

She focussed her attention on the Christmas market that had completely taken over the village on Jewel Island over the last few days. She'd been on the island since the start of December and when she'd arrived there hadn't been anything on the village green, then slowly the Christmas market had started to take shape. The large wooden huts had been delivered and built in the first week, then all the lights and decorations had gone up too, twinkling strings strewn across the roofs with decorated Christmas trees in between the wooden lodges. There was a large amount of fake snow everywhere; obviously the organisers had known the weather would let them down. Over the last week all the stall holders had moved in en-masse with their Christmassy wares that sparkled and glittered from the front of each of the wooden lodges. It looked magical. There were candles, snow globes, bath bombs, Christmas ornaments, jewellery, scarves, Christmas jumpers, sweets, chutneys and jams and a whole assortment of Christmas foods, chocolates and cakes. Next door to her, a lovely Finnish woman called Marika was selling the most amazing gingerbread biscuits and what looked like star-shaped jam tarts made from puff pastry, called joulutorttu, which she was dying to taste. She couldn't wait to have a look around at all the stalls but she knew she would be tempted to try almost all of the food that was on offer in the lead-up to the big day.

Zoey felt a tiny bit of a fraud with her market stand amongst all the Christmas wonders, because her wares weren't really Christmassy at all. She was an artist, painting small seaside village landscapes with their quirky houses and interesting characters. She had spent the last few weeks painting her landscapes with Christmas trees, snow and her villagers wearing Santa hats to try to inject a bit of the festivities into her paintings and justify her place here in the market.

It had been her mum, Beth's, idea for Zoey to run a stand at the Christmas market on Jewel Island, in the furthest reaches of Cornwall. Mainly because her mum had moved to the island six months before and was desperate for Zoey to come down and spend some time over Christmas with her. And with Zoey's ex-fiancé getting ready to marry the love of his life in Copper Tree, the little town where she lived, in a big Christmas Eve wedding, it seemed a good time to escape.

It wasn't that she still loved David. It had actually been something of a relief to walk in on him going at it with his work colleague, Vicky, like his life depended on it ten months before. She'd had a feeling for a while that something just wasn't right between them so she was glad she'd found out before their big day. The thing that bothered her was that the wedding between him and Vicky was technically her wedding, which was more than a little weird. After the subsequent break-up, Zoey had left the cancellations of all their wedding plans down to him, except, not one to ever inconvenience himself, he'd never done it. Instead he had simply switched Zoey's name for Vicky's. The venue they'd chosen, the menus they'd tasted and decided upon, even the honeymoon on an island in Scotland with glass igloos to watch the Northern Lights had stayed exactly the same. The bridesmaids, David's sisters, were still wearing the same red dresses. The only thing different was that Vicky had decided on her own wedding

3

dress. David had done the decent thing, bought Zoey out of her share of the wedding and the house – or rather his parents had, to make sure that Zoey was expunged from their son's life once and for all – and Zoey had been only too pleased to leave that part of her life behind. But she wasn't the only one who thought it was strange. Every time she went into the town or into a shop, people would come up to her and ask her if she was OK with it. Which of course she wasn't, it was creepy as hell. She needed a break and a month on Jewel Island working in a beautiful Christmas market and time spent with her mum sounded like the perfect remedy.

Beth had wanted Zoey to stay with her in her new house, but as it had only one bedroom and the best her mum could offer was the tiny two-seater sofa, Zoey had decided to stay at the Sapphire Bay Hotel instead. As luck would have it they had one of their self-catering cottages in the hotel grounds available for the whole month of December and she was now staying in a tiny cottage over-looking Moonstone Lake, which was very beautiful and quiet. Zoey could get used to life on Jewel Island; it was a slower way of life here, peaceful. All the islanders she'd met were so friendly and welcoming.

Zoey and her mum had always talked about one day living by the sea, they'd seen pictures of cottages with sea views and they'd imagined themselves there, listening to the waves lap against the shore, going for long walks on the beach, enjoying the quiet and solitude that growing up in London never afforded them. Even when Zoey had grown up they'd talked about it as the ideal dream. Zoey had often found herself looking at estate agent listings by the coast, finding the perfect house that one day she would move into. Her paintings were of little seaside villages and, whenever she visited coastal towns for inspiration, she always imagined herself living there. And while she hadn't come to Jewel Island with the view of moving here, now she could picture herself here very easily. A few days before the market had officially opened, Zoey had even found herself looking in the estate agent's window at houses for sale or rent. There was a little house available right on the harbour with a small balcony overlooking the sea. One bedroom, kitchen lounge and dining room all in one, but surprisingly it had quite a large garden. She could get a lot of inspiration for her paintings living there, sitting on the balcony watching the world go by. And with her mum now living here it kind of made sense to be closer to her. She loved Copper Tree and its people but maybe it was time to make a clean break, move on once and for all.

Marika came back from her wander around the Christmas market with a big smile on her face, clutching a mug of what looked like hot mulled wine.

'I found glögi,' Marika said, excitedly. 'Elias from number eighteen is selling it, he's from Finland too but much much further north than I am. He says the English call it mulled wine, but it's definitely glögi. Do you want to try some?'

Marika offered out the steaming mug towards her and Zoey wrapped her hands around it and took a sip.

'Mmm, this is delicious.'

Marika nodded enthusiastically. 'There's a lot of fruit in glögi. Some places use blueberries, some use strawberries and blackcurrants, and spices of course, and then it's mixed with the red wine and heated. Or you can have alcohol-free ones, which are just as nice because you can really taste the fruit more.'

Zoey took another tiny quick sip and felt it warm her from the inside. 'I could really get used to this.'

She passed it back to Marika before she was tempted to drink the whole thing.

'Traditionally, glögi is served with gingerbread biscuits so we've agreed to do a discount for our customers. Whenever I sell some biscuits, I will tell my customers that it's traditionally eaten with a glass of glögi and if they go to Elias and tell him I sent them, he'll give them ten percent off the glögi, and he will do the same for me to send his customers my way.'

'What a wonderful idea,' Zoey said.

Marika nodded and then glanced around surreptitiously. 'He's pretty cute too, so it's no hardship to have an arrangement with him.'

Zoey laughed.

'You should go and have a look around, the place is wonderful and each stall has something different. I'll keep an eye on your stall for you.'

Zoey wanted to see the market for herself. The opening weekend had been so busy with all the tourists and locals coming to see the first Christmas market on Jewel Island that she hadn't had a chance to look around or leave her hut, but as today was Monday it was a little bit quieter. She knew it would probably pick up again later when people finished work. The thing with selling paintings was there was never a steady stream of customers, unlike for Marika's gingerbread biscuits or the cakes and crêpes and churros. People would come in and look at her pictures and say how wonderful they were and how cute they would look in the kitchen or the lounge and then wander off again. Buying a painting for the house felt like a big commitment for some people, and the originals were always just a bit too pricey for the average tourist, so she didn't feel like she was going to miss out on the sale of the century if she had a wander round for a while.

'Thanks Marika, the price is on everything. The two paintings in the gold frames are not for sale.'

Marika nodded, ushering her out. 'Go and check out the cakes at number twelve and the cutest tree ornaments with Constance at number thirty-seven. There's a man selling fancy dress costumes for Christmas, so if you fancy dressing up as Santa or even a sexy Mrs Santa, he's your man. And if you get a glass of glögi, Elias is selling it way too hot. I told him. So walk around a bit and let it cool down before you take a sip otherwise you'll burn your mouth. And you must go to number twenty-three. Kit is lovely and his churros are amazing.'

'I will, thanks,' Zoey said, smiling at the list of instructions. She moved out of her hut and started wandering through the market. There was a buzz of excitement and happiness in the air as people mooched around the stalls buying presents for friends and family or treating themselves. People were trying new and exciting foods and drinks and generally just enjoying getting into the festive spirit.

There was a stall selling Christmas jumpers of every design and pattern. There were reindeer and puddings, rude ones and cute ones, ones with characters from

Batman and Star Wars, unicorns and dinosaurs with a hint of Christmas. There was even one with Jesus on the front wearing a Santa hat with the words, 'It's my birthday'. The wide selection made Zoey's white jumper with a glittery owl wearing a Santa hat on the front seem a bit tame in comparison. She knew she'd have to buy her mum one, she loved getting a new Christmas jumper every year.

The food smelt amazing and her stomach rumbled appreciatively. Spotting the stall that sold the glögi she went over and ordered herself a mug. As Marika said, it was clearly way too hot so she moved away to let it cool down just as three boys charged through the market chasing each other with water pistols. She'd heard the local school had closed early due to a fault with the heating so the kids were obviously trying to occupy themselves here. One barged into her before running off, knocking her mug of glögi out of her hands and all over her. She had a fleeting second while she stared at the red stain all over her white jumper in disappointment before she felt how burning hot it was as it seeped onto her skin.

Without thinking, she ripped her jumper off, realising a split second after she'd done so that she'd managed to yank her t-shirt off in the process, so she was standing there only in her bra. A second later a bucket of cold water was thrown over her.

She stood there dripping in a state of shock for a moment, blinking the water out of her eyes before she registered there was a man in front of her, holding an empty bucket and looking aghast.

'Oh my god, I'm so sorry,' the man said. 'I panicked when I saw you get covered in that hot mulled wine.'

'So you threw a bucket of water over me? I wasn't on fire.'

'I know, it seemed like a good idea at the time.'

It had actually seemed to have done the trick. The jumper hadn't been on her long enough to cause any damage so, while her skin still felt tender, she wasn't in any real pain. She realised people were starting to stare; a few had grabbed their mobile phones and begun filming. She quickly held her jumper up in front of herself, embarrassment flooding her cheeks.

The man looked round and realised the problem too. 'Come with me.'

He grabbed her hand and marched back towards one of the huts, one that sold crêpes and churros. There were people in there too, staring with open mouths, but the man led her past them into the small storage area out the back. He swiftly closed the door separating them from the rest of the shop.

'Are you OK?' His eyes were filled with concern.

'Soaking wet, embarrassed beyond belief, pissed off that my favourite jumper is ruined, but, apart from that, I'm fine.' She wrung her hair out, noticing the jaunty name badge that said his name was Kit. 'Although I guess I should say thank you for your quick thinking.'

'I am sorry. I had a cup of that stuff earlier, it's boiling hot. I burnt my arm once, dropped scalding soup over it, I've never felt pain like it. My skin blistered up in seconds and I had the most horrific burn on my skin for months. I'd hate for anyone to go through that.'

'That sounds horrible. Were you in pain for long?'

Kit shook his head. 'I wrapped cling film around my

arm, that took the pain away instantly.' His eyes scanned down her body briefly. 'I think we'd need quite a bit of cling film if we were to wrap your whole body.' His eyes widened in horror. 'I don't mean that I think you're fat, far from it, just that a body would need more cling film than an arm would. Christ, how to make a bad situation worse. I'm so sorry.'

Zoey couldn't help but laugh. 'Don't worry.'

He quickly turned away to rummage through his bag. 'I have a spare t-shirt in here – it's clean, I promise. You can take that.'

Kit handed her a t-shirt and she held it out in front of her. The t-shirt had multiple pictures of snowmen in various sex positions.

'Interesting,' Zoey said.

'Oh shit, sorry,' Kit said. 'My brother, Adam, gave it to me. His idea of a joke because he says I've been single too long.'

Zoey turned it inside out and then pulled it on. 'Problem solved.'

Kit shook his head, ruefully. 'And this is why I've been single too long. I throw buckets of water over beautiful women, call them fat and give them rude t-shirts.'

She smiled. He was a good-looking guy in a dishevelled kind of way, with dark rumpled hair, a bit of stubble that was bordering between deliberately sexy and that got-out-of-bed-too-late-to-shave style. His t-shirt under his apron was creased, the apron itself was stained with splatters of chocolate. But he had gentle grey eyes and a nice smile. His shoulders were large and toned, his arms looked sturdy and safe.

'There are better ways of getting a woman's attention. You could just ask them out,' Zoey said.

His eyes widened. 'You want to go out with me after all that?'

She blushed. 'I didn't mean me. Just women in general.'

His shoulders dropped a little. 'Of course not you.'

Now she felt bad for him. 'Look, I think we got off on the wrong foot. I'm Zoey Flynn from number nine.'

'Kit Lewis,' the man said and offered out his hand. She shook it.

'See, now we're friends. If you want to seal the deal how about you do me a bag of those churros I've heard so much about?'

His face lit up. 'You've heard about my churros?'

'Marika runs the stall next to mine, she said your churros were amazing.'

'Oh, that's nice.'

They were still holding hands and she smiled because he didn't seem to realise, he was too busy staring at her with a smile.

'You have the most incredible eyes,' Kit said, softly. 'They're holly green.'

Her heart leapt at the compliment. 'Thank you. Now that's the kind of thing you say to impress a woman. If you'd led with that instead of the bucket of water, I'd have been putty in your hands.'

'I don't think me running up to you to give you a compliment about your eyes as you got third-degree burns would have been great timing.'

'No, probably not.'

He stared at her for a moment. 'Is it too late?'

'For what?'

'Putty?'

She smiled. 'Not necessarily. Let's see how amazing these churros really are.'

'Wow, now I feel there's a lot riding on these churros,' Kit said, suddenly realising he was still holding her hand. He quickly let her go. 'Sorry. Let's get you those churros quick before I do anything else to scare you away.'

He walked out into the main shop area and she followed him, noticing for the first time there was a young woman serving the crêpes.

There was a small queue waiting to be served the churros and Zoey watched as Kit flashed a winning smile at them.

'Sorry, won't keep you a moment,' he said.

He piped five long fingers of batter into the large pan of hot oil, cutting each one off when they got to the desired length. He gave the hot chocolate sauce a stir as the churros quickly cooked, then scooped them out and rolled them in the sugar and cinnamon, before popping them in a small tray and pouring the hot chocolate sauce into a separate section in the corner of the tray.

He passed them to Zoey and she immediately fished her purse out of her pocket but he waved it away.

'Please, after throwing a bucket of water all over you, I think this is the least I can do.' He gestured for her to try one.

She took one and dipped it into the hot chocolate sauce and took a bite. 'Mmm, these really are amazing.'

'Amazing enough for... putty?'

'Kit, you've got customers,' the woman said, clearly a bit annoyed at being left to man the fort.

'I should probably go. Why don't you come and see me later and we can talk about... putty,' Zoey said.

He smiled. 'OK, I will.'

She walked out of the hut and down the path between the other stalls but, when she looked back at Kit's hut, he was standing there watching her go.

CHAPTER 2

Zoey was just closing her hut up for the night when she noticed Kit approaching her carrying a bag. Her heart leapt when she saw him; there was something just so endearing about him.

'Hello,' Zoey said. 'Have you come to talk to me about putty?'

He laughed. 'Maybe I can do better than that. I've bought you a present.'

'Oh, thank you.'

He passed her the bag and she opened it to see a Christmas jumper inside.

'To make up for the one you ruined,' Kit said.

'Thank you,' she said, pulling it out of the bag to have a look at it. 'That's really…' she trailed off because the red jumper had a small Christmas pudding on it, right at the bottom of the jumper so it would sit directly over her belly. Written in italic white writing were the words, 'My little pudding'. This was obviously a jumper for a pregnant lady, the pudding being a reference to the baby bump.

Zoey had never really considered herself overweight before. She wasn't thin by any standards, but her belly was reasonably flat. However, it was hard not to be offended by this. Did Kit think she was pregnant? There was the comment before about using lots of cling film to wrap up her body. She'd probably put on a pound or two in recent weeks with all the glorious Christmas chocolate she'd been snacking on but she'd also been running a lot more to make up for it.

'Do you like it?' Kit said, eagerly. 'Some of those jumpers were quite rude, and I didn't want a repeat of the t-shirt with the snowmen having sex. The guy who owned the stall was closing up so I had to be quick. Thought a Christmas pudding was quite safe.'

Oh god, he had no idea. And she couldn't tell him because buying her a Christmas jumper was a really lovely gesture, even if she would have preferred one with a pudding slightly higher up.

She cleared her throat. 'It's lovely, thank you.'

'I'm glad you like it. So I was wondering if you wanted to go and grab a drink or a bite to eat tonight?' Kit said really quickly as if he'd been psyching himself up to say it.

She couldn't help smiling. He was asking her out. It had been a long time since anyone had asked her out. It was a funny situation living in the same town as her ex. She had moved to Copper Tree once she and David had got engaged and had loved the little rural town with its friendly locals and views over the fields, so when they'd broken up she'd moved into a flat in the same place. But being David's ex, someone who was hugely popular with everyone in the town, she'd somehow been tainted as if it was her fault he'd been cheating on her. No one had asked her out in the ten months since they'd broken up, no one had even flirted with her. Although that might have had more to do with the fact she'd put out vibes that said she wasn't interested in a relationship any more, she was happy on her own. Though Kit didn't know that. She looked at him, his beautiful eyes filled with hope. Was it time to make a new start in other aspects of her life too? Could she start dating again?

'I can't tonight,' Zoey said.

His face fell a little though he was clearly trying to keep his smile plastered on it. 'That's OK, no problem, some other time maybe. Have a good night.'

He started to move off and she snagged his arm. 'No, I genuinely can't, I'm having dinner with my mum. But if you're hungry you're more than welcome to come along.'

'Oh,' he clearly thought about it for a moment.

It was probably a bit weird asking him to come to dinner with her mum when they hadn't even gone out on a date yet. But she wasn't sure if it would ever get that far with Kit. There was a definite attraction but she got the feeling that while she could be good friends with him, she wasn't sure if she was ready for something more. She was enjoying not being in a relationship right now, taking time just for her. She certainly hadn't come to Jewel Island looking for love.

'Well, if your mum won't mind, that would be great,' Kit said. 'It gets a bit lonely sitting in the hotel restaurant every night. My sister, Lindsey, the woman helping me make crêpes, she lives nearby and invites me round sometimes but I do feel like the third wheel with her and her boyfriend.'

'You'd be very welcome, Mum always makes too much food anyway. I'll just text her to let her know you're coming.'

She pulled her phone from her bag and sent a quick message saying she was bringing a friend.

'She doesn't live far, just up here behind the school.'

They started walking away from the village green towards the houses at one end.

Zoey shivered a little. She was only wearing Kit's t-shirt under her coat as her jumper was still damp and stained from her earlier misadventure with the glögi.

'Are you cold? You could put your new jumper on,' Kit said.

Zoey cleared her throat. 'Yes I could.'

She shrugged out of her coat and pulled the Christmas pudding jumper on. Her mum was going to go nuts over this jumper, Zoey had to warn her.

She pulled her coat back on and grabbed her phone again and quickly wrote another text, although her mum was yet to reply to the first one. *Please don't mention the jumper.*

She slipped her phone back into her pocket as they continued walking to her mum's house. 'So, making crêpes and churros, is that what you do for a living or is it more saving damsels in distress?'

He laughed. 'Thank God I'm not responsible for saving anyone, you can see how bad I'd be at it. I know a little first aid, so if you cut your finger I could give you a plaster, but that's about it. Crêpes and churros are more of a hobby. I love it and I love the happiness something as simple as a hot churro in chocolate sauce can bring someone. It's something I always used to do for my niece and nephews when they came to stay and they love them, so when the local animal shelter was holding a fundraising day I thought it might be something I could offer them. My churros were a hit so it's something I do from time to time. It gives me a bit of spending money and I love doing it, but it's not my real job. I, umm… draw cartoon strips for a living.'

'Oh my god, what a cool job,' Zoey said. 'For a newspaper or in a comic?'

'Both actually. I draw for *The Comet*.'

'Oh wow, that's a great gig to draw for them. I get that paper from time to time, there's a great comic strip about a fox and a badger. Brian and Bert. It's so funny, it's always the first thing I read whenever I buy the paper.'

'Well I'm glad you find it funny,' Kit said, brushing his hand through his hair awkwardly.

'That's you? You draw Brian and Bert? I love them!'

'Thank you.'

'How do you do it? Write such funny stories in four little pictures?'

'I don't know, they're easy characters to work with. There's so much comedy potential with a moaning old badger and fox. They've been there and seen it all. I draw for *The Village* too, but we have a team of writers who come up with the gags and storylines, and I'm part of a team of artists who illustrates them. It's a different way of working.'

'Sounds interesting.'

'It is, it's fun. I also do designs for birthday cards for extra money and I've illustrated a few children's books too.'

'That's wonderful.'

'Really, you think so?'

'Yes, I think it's great to make a living doing something you love.'

They passed Seamus, the village mayor, and his chunky dog, Chew Barker, out for a walk. Zoey's mum had already made a point of introducing her to many of the locals and she'd met Seamus and his wife Kathy on the first day she was here. He was a lovely man. In fact, everyone she had met so far had been lovely. Seamus looked like he wanted to be back inside, warming his feet by the fire, while Chew Barker looked like he could stay outside all night finding all the sniffs. Seamus flashed them a smile as he hurried by.

They passed cute little thatched cottages, with twinkling lights in the windows and elaborate holly wreaths on the front doors. Zoey realised that Kit was deep in thought, his eyebrows drawn down in a tiny frown.

'My ex-wife hated that I was a cartoonist, she thought it was childish.'

'Oh no, I'm sorry. I think some people don't understand those that are creative. I'm an artist too – ink, watercolour and acrylics – and a lot of people think it's just a silly hobby rather than something that actually pays the bills. And art is so subjective too, some people look at my drawings and think they are too childlike or silly for their tastes, but others love them and that's all that matters. It doesn't pay really well, I get big commissions sometimes and I might sell originals to hotels or restaurants, that's always good money, but that doesn't happen as often as I'd like, so I do birthday and Christmas cards too. I have my paintings printed on mugs, bags, scarves, stuff like that, and I sell it on Etsy and Not on the High Street. I make a living but I haven't bought the big flashy Porsche yet.'

Kit laughed. 'No, mine's on hold too. I mean, I get a regular wage from my work with the newspapers, so that's nice, but it's certainly not a glamorous life. What kind of stuff do you paint?'

'Village landscapes, quirky stuff, someone falling off a ladder one side of a village, a secret lover escaping out of a window on the other side. One of those paintings that the more you look at it, the more you see, and if you don't properly look at it, you still get a nice quirky seaside village picture.'

'I know exactly what you mean. My dad used to paint village scenes,' Kit said. 'I love that kind of thing. I'll have to come round tomorrow and have a look.'

They passed a mother and teenage daughter carrying a tree into their tiny cottage. It looked way too big to fit in there, but the daughter was clearly delighted with it.

Zoey smiled at the mother.

'Do you live locally?' Kit asked Zoey.

'I live about an hour and a half away from here, a little countryside town called Copper Tree, but… I'm thinking about moving here. My mum's here and I'm at a stage of my life where I feel I need a change. I've been here since the start of December and I love it. The sea views from almost anywhere on the island are amazing. It has always been my dream to live in a house by the sea. I even started looking at properties the other day. There's a cute house I saw in the estate agent window, overlooking the harbour. I could really see myself living there.'

'The one with the blue kitchen cabinets and the wrought-iron balcony? Yes, I saw that too the other day,' Kit said.

'Are you looking to move as well? Is that why you were looking in the estate agent window too?'

'I hadn't really thought about moving house until recently, but I'm still in the rented house I shared with my ex-wife in Bath and I've started to think it feels like it's time for a new start. I work from home so I can work anywhere and there's something wonderful and peaceful about Jewel Island.'

'We could end up as neighbours,' Zoey said.

'Or housemates as we were both looking at the same house,' Kit pointed out.

'Sadly that house only has one bedroom, which might make for a slightly awkward house-share arrangement.'

'That's true.'

They walked up the path of her mum's cottage and Zoey used her key to open the front door. She called out to her mum. After a few moments her mum came hurrying through from the kitchen to greet them.

'Hello my lovely, come on in.' Beth hugged her warmly and ushered her inside. 'Oh, who's this?'

'This is Kit, a friend from the market. I did text you to let you know I was bringing him,' Zoey said. 'Kit, this is my mum, Beth.'

'It's a pleasure to meet you,' Kit said, holding out his hand, but Beth pulled him into a big hug too.

Zoey unzipped her coat.

'Any friend of Zoey's is more than welcome,' Beth said.

'Did you get my text?' Zoey said, suddenly not wanting to take her coat off and reveal her jumper. If her mum hadn't seen the message to say Kit was coming she wouldn't have seen the message about the jumper either.

'Oh, I have no idea where my phone is, it might be in the loo, but it doesn't matter, there's plenty of food.'

Zoey's heart sank; this was not going to go well.

'Come on, take your coats off, come on inside the kitchen and I'll get you a drink,' Beth said, holding her hands out to take their coats.

Kit passed her his coat and Zoey reluctantly took hers off and passed it to her mum too, trying to convey with her eyes to her mum that she wasn't to react to the jumper. It would go one of two ways: Beth would see the jumper and laugh at her wearing it, knowing she couldn't possibly be pregnant, which would make Kit feel bad for getting the wrong jumper, or—

'Oh my god you're pregnant!' Beth squealed, throwing her arms around Zoey and holding her tight. 'I'm so happy, why didn't you tell me?'

'Mum—'

Beth turned her attention to Kit, pulling him into another big hug. 'Congratulations Kit, you must be over the moon.' She looked back at Zoey resting her hands on her non-existent bump. 'How far along are you? Have you been to see the doctor? Have you had your scan? I didn't even know you were seeing anyone. Have you thought about names? Oh god, this is the best news ever. I'm going to be a granny. And this is how you chose to tell me the good news. This jumper is so cute. Let me get a picture of the two of you.'

Kit was looking like he wanted to run a mile as Beth hurried off to get her camera. 'You're pregnant?'

'No, of course not.'

'Then why does she think you are?'

Zoey sighed. 'Because the jumper you bought me is a maternity one. The Christmas pudding being a reference to the baby bump. It even says, "My little pudding".'

He stared at her in horror. 'I thought it just meant *my pudding*, I didn't realise it meant a baby. Bloody hell, they should really advertise these things more clearly. I can't believe I bought you a maternity jumper. Why didn't you tell me?'

'I didn't want to upset you.'

'Christ!'

Beth came back with her camera and her smile stretching from ear to ear. 'Now stand together, put your arm round her.'

'Mum, I'm sorry, I'm not pregnant.'

Beth's face fell. 'You're not?'

'Kit and I just met today, I spilt hot mulled wine down my jumper, Kit bought me this as a replacement. He didn't realise it was a maternity jumper and I didn't have the heart to tell him. I did send you a text to warn you, but sadly it seems you didn't get it.'

'Oh no.' Beth stared at the pudding longingly and then slowly a smile spread on her face. 'You bought her a maternity jumper? That's hilarious.'

Poor Kit blushed as red as a tomato.

Her mum was almost howling.

'Mum, stop,' Zoey said, the laughter bubbling inside her too. 'It was really sweet.'

But then Kit was laughing too, shaking his head. 'See, this is why I'm single.'

'I don't know, being able to laugh at yourself is a very good quality to have,' Zoey said.

'Plus you're cute,' Beth said. 'A lot of girls would go for that. Come on into the kitchen and you can tell me about the market.'

She moved off through the door at the end of the hall, still laughing.

Kit sighed. 'I am sorry.'

Zoey grinned and slid her hand into his giving it a brief squeeze before letting it go. 'Don't worry about it. If we ever get married, this can be one of those funny things we tell the grandkids.'

He smiled and she ushered him down to the kitchen.

Kit smiled to himself about how his day had gone. After working so hard over the last week to get his hut ready for the big opening weekend, he'd ended up oversleeping that morning. He'd turned up over an hour late, which had thrilled his sister no end, especially as she'd been in a bad mood anyway after a silly row with her boyfriend. The morning had been busy with a steady stream of customers, which was good, so he hadn't had a proper chance to have a look around the market.

And then there was Zoey, her chestnut hair glowing like bronze in the winter sun, her pale skin with a smattering of freckles across her cheeks and nose, blowing on her mug of mulled wine. She'd looked enchanting.

And then he'd thrown a bucket of water over her, implied she was fat, given her a t-shirt with snowmen having sex and then a maternity jumper. It wasn't the best start. Yet, he was here, playing Pictionary with Zoey and her mum and he couldn't be happier. What had started out as a bit of a crappy day had turned out to be pretty bloody great.

He and Zoey just clicked in a way he'd never experienced before. He had no idea whether anything was going to happen between them. He got the distinct impression that she saw him as a friend, or she wasn't interested in anything more, but actually he was more than OK with that. Zoey was the kind of special person he wanted in his life and if that meant just being friends, then he'd take that over not having her at all. Besides, his confidence had taken a battering after his divorce and he'd not been with a woman since his wife had left him for another man. Getting involved in a relationship laid himself wide open to getting hurt and he wasn't sure he was ready for that yet.

Kit watched as Zoey laughed so hard at her mum's attempts at drawing that she could hardly breathe. The sand on the timer was nearly running out and Beth had managed to draw two triangles with curved bottoms either side of two long straight vertical lines joined at the top with a squiggle which she was pointing to frantically. There were actions too, which was probably not allowed in the rules of Pictionary. She was doing the classic catalogue pose of looking for something and then pointing to the triangles and the squiggly part of the line. Zoey had tears running down her cheeks.

'As lovely as it would be to let you continue this for another few minutes, time is up, I'm afraid,' Kit said.

Beth's shoulders dropped. 'Oh but you were so close to guessing it.'

'Mum, if we had another hour, I don't think we would have guessed it,' Zoey said.

'But it's obvious, isn't it? It's a lighthouse,' Beth said, gesturing to the stalk with the squiggle.

This made Zoey laugh even louder and he couldn't help but smile as he watched her.

'How is it a lighthouse?' Zoey said.

'Wait, are those triangles supposed to be boats?' Kit said.

'Yes, of course they are.' Beth was clearly a little bit miffed that they hadn't guessed it.

'Ah, now I know they're boats, of course I can see it's a lighthouse,' Kit said, reassuringly.

Beth let out a noise of frustration. 'We can't all be gifted artists, you know.'

'It was a… good effort,' Zoey said and gave her mum's arm an affectionate squeeze.

Beth rolled her eyes and smiled with love for her daughter. 'I'm not playing Pictionary with you two again.'

'I think your talents lie elsewhere, like cooking. Those meatballs tonight were delicious and the banana cake was amazing,' Zoey said.

'I agree. I've never tasted anything like it,' Kit said.

Beth was clearly very easily won around, a smile appearing on her face. 'Go on with you.'

Zoey stood up. 'Well on that note, it's getting late and I think we better go. We both have to get up early tomorrow to open up our stalls.'

'Well, it's been lovely having you both here.' Beth stood up too. 'I might pop down to the market tomorrow and have a look around.'

'If you come to see me, I'll give you complimentary churros,' Kit said.

'I might take you up on that,' Beth said, following them out to the door and handing them their coats. She smiled again at the jumper Zoey was wearing. 'You definitely need to keep that jumper, it will make me smile every time I see it.'

'Then I'll absolutely keep it. I'll wear it on Christmas Day.'

'Oh yes, you must. Kit, what are your plans for the big day? You'd be very welcome to come here. I might even let you play Pictionary again,' Beth said.

Kit didn't have great Christmas plans. His brother, Adam, and his wife were taking their kids to his wife's family for Christmas and his sister and her boyfriend were flying out to Austria early Christmas Eve. He'd been thinking he might try to crash one of his friends' celebrations but he suddenly found that he couldn't think of a better way to spend Christmas than with Zoey and her wonderful mum.

'I'd really like that. Thank you.'

Beth hugged her daughter and then gave Kit a big warm hug too.

After a few more goodbyes, they were out on the street, Zoey doing up her coat.

'Are you staying at the hotel too?' Kit said.

'Yes, sort of. I'm in one of the hotel's cottages in the grounds right next to Moonstone Lake.'

'Oh, nice, I'll walk you back if you like.'

She smiled. 'That's not necessary. The island is very safe.'

'Well if you're that brave, you can walk me back. I get scared of the dark.'

She laughed and then, to his delight, she slipped her hand into his. 'I'll look after you.'

Her hand was warm as she entwined her fingers with his and he felt his smile spread across his face.

The night was cold, their breath causing little billows of steam in the air. The snow had stopped falling and there was a tiny dusting on the ground, making the world sparkle in the moonlight.

'Your mum is wonderful,' Kit said, because it was the truth.

'She is. I'm totally biased of course, but I think she's bloody amazing.'

'I agree.'

'I never had a dad, so she did both jobs when I was growing up and I can promise you I never missed out.'

'I don't doubt that. What happened to Dad?'

He felt her hand tighten instinctively. 'He was a shitbag who treated Mum appallingly. Her own parents had quite a volatile relationship and I think that shaped her opinion of what a relationship should be. She had quite a few crappy relationships and then met the man who biologically is my father. They'd been going out eleven months when he hit her for the first and last time. She packed her bags and left.

Then she found out she was pregnant with me. In her mind there was never any question of letting him be a part of my life when he treated her so badly. She was so scared he'd find her, she changed her name and his name isn't mentioned on the birth certificate. I have no idea who he is and have no desire to find out. As I said, I certainly didn't miss out by just being raised by my mum.'

'I'm so sorry your mum went through that,' Kit said.

Zoey nodded. 'It made her realise she could do it on her own. In some ways I feel grateful that he showed his true colours before they got married or before I came along, so she could get out before she was tied to him forever. She is a brave and brilliant woman and he taught her that she was better off alone than being with him.'

'And there wasn't anyone else, no boyfriends, no stepdads?'

'No stepdads. She had a few dates here and there but nothing serious. But there was a lovely guy, our neighbour, who moved next door when I was around eight or nine. They became really good friends. He was so good for her, good for me too, I suppose. He made her so happy. He also taught me how to paint, which I'll forever be grateful for. He had such a patient way about him. He was very gentle. Sadly he died when I was nineteen. There was never anyone else of significance.'

'I'm glad your mum had someone who treated her right, who made her happy.'

'I am too.' They were silent for a while then she spoke. 'What about your parents, divorced, together or…?'

'They both died, several years ago. Dad went first when I was twenty, Mum went a few years after that. She was never the same after he'd gone. They'd been together all their lives, best friends as teenagers before they started dating, they were married by twenty. They gave me a great example of what love should be. I think real love, the kind that lasts, has good friendship at its core. I think you have to take the time to get to know someone before you can count on forever. They had that. They were so completely in love with each other, it broke her heart when he died.'

'I'm so sorry,' Zoey said. 'That must have been so hard to lose them both.'

'It was and I'm the eldest of three so it felt like I had to carry the family in some way. I mean, they were both adults when Mum passed away so it's not like I had to look after them but it felt like it was down to me to sort everything out.'

'It doesn't seem fair when you are supposed to be taking the time to grieve for your parents that there's so much paperwork and things to sort out. There should be some kind of service that would take care of all of that for you.'

'I'd definitely pay for that.'

'And your dad used to paint too, is that where you learned?' Zoey said.

He smiled that she'd remembered that from their conversation earlier. 'He was certainly the person that sparked that love of drawing and painting in me. We used to draw together and I loved that, but our styles were very different. He always gave me so much encouragement though, even for my little doodles. That's why I started getting into cartoon strips, making something out of simple doodles and sketches. Dad loved them.'

She smiled at him. 'Sounds like you had a lot of support.'

'I did, from both of them. Though Mum's support was more cheerleading than teaching.'

'I know what you mean. Mum kept every drawing and painting I did as a child. She put them all in scrapbooks which she still keeps in a big box in the loft. Anyone would think she's proud of me,' Zoey smirked.

'I think it's very clear she's proud of you,' Kit said.

They walked back through the Christmas market, which was empty at this time of night, though the Christmas lights were still twinkling away in the darkness.

'Isn't it so pretty,' Zoey said. 'I love Christmas, it's my favourite time of year. I love the decorations and the festive foods and scents. It makes me so happy. Mum always used to make the day so magical when I was a child with sparkly reindeer food and special Christmas cookies that had come straight from the North Pole. I was always allowed to stay up till midnight on Christmas Day to make a Christmas wish.'

'What's the Christmas wish?'

'On the stroke of midnight, the last few seconds of Christmas Day, you make a wish and because there's still so much Christmas magic floating around there's more chance of it coming true.'

'I like that. Well, for children, of course.'

'Hey, just because we're adults doesn't mean we can't enjoy a little Christmas magic.'

She looked up at him and must have seen him pull a face because her own face dropped.

'Don't tell me you're one of those Christmas haters?' Zoey said, aghast.

'I don't hate Christmas. I suppose it seems like a lot of fuss for one day.' He smiled as he remembered his Christmases growing up. 'I used to love it as a child. It just doesn't mean as much any more. Mum and Dad used to make it so special for us too, we'd make mince pies, decorate the tree together, make Christmas cake, we'd go and see the lights in our local town, watch a pantomime every year – it was wonderful spending time together. But since they've both died it hasn't been the same. We're rarely together at Christmas any more. My brother is married with children and they usually spend Christmas round his wife's parents. My sister always tends to go away for Christmas, with her boyfriend or friends. Christmas was always such a big deal in our house that I think it hurts too much to celebrate it without our parents.'

'What do you do at Christmas if you haven't got family to spend it with?'

'Normally just crash a friend's celebrations, whichever friend is most amenable to me turning up on the big day.'

'Oh, I'm sorry.'

He shook his head with a smile. 'It's OK, I'm not really big on Christmas, not any more. I'm quite happy having a curry and watching crappy Christmas TV or films. It doesn't bother me if I'm alone.'

'Well you won't be alone this year.'

He smiled. 'Thank you. I'm looking forward to it.'

They were quiet for a while as they entered the hotel grounds, which were lit up with a trail of fairy lights and illuminated Christmas trees leading up to the main entrance. The hotel stood tall and bright above them, a large white building with big windows, giving guests an amazing view over the sea.

'So do all your first dates start off at your mum's house?' Kit asked.

Zoey laughed. 'I'm not sure this can really count as a first date.'

Kit nodded. He'd thought as much. They had talked and laughed a lot that night but she definitely hadn't been flirting with him, which was a shame. Zoey was the kind of person he could really fall for but now it seemed they were heading straight for the friendzone.

'Although if it was, I think you definitely passed the mum test. She adored you,' she said.

He smiled. 'Well, that's nice.'

'I'm up this way if you want to insist on walking me back,' Zoey gestured to a path that went up the hill.

'Well, I certainly don't want to lose any Mum brownie points by letting you walk back on your own.'

'No, Mum brownie points are precious.'

They started walking up the hill. There were a few lights illuminating the path but not so many as in the main gardens. The stars and the moon looked so much brighter here without any streetlights to dilute them.

'I haven't dated anyone since I broke up with my ex ten months ago. Not because he broke my heart, I think it was over between us long before then, but sometimes you just need a break from relationships for a while before you plunge headfirst into another one.'

And here was the speech where she told him she only wanted to be friends. He'd heard that speech before but for some reason he felt more disappointed about this one. But he couldn't blame her for feeling that way. He'd been where she was now. He was probably still there, truth be told. His marriage hadn't ended well and there hadn't been anyone for him since. He wasn't sure he was ready for a relationship again either.

They approached Moonstone Lake, which glittered with the thick layer of ice on top of it. A tiny cottage sat alone on the shore, a golden light from the window casting a warm glow across the ground in front of the cottage. From up here, they could see the whole island laid out beneath them, the hotel with lights burning from every window, the twinkling lights of the village and the sea beyond glittering in the moonlight.

Zoey looked up at him and he got the feeling she wanted to let him down gently. He didn't want things to be awkward between them. He decided to change the subject.

'What a beautiful place to spend the holidays,' Kit said.

A movement on the lake caught his eye and he realised a rabbit was slipping and sliding over the icy surface as it desperately tried to get back to the edge.

'Oh shit,' he said, pointing to the frantic creature.

'Oh no,' Zoey said.

He let go of her hand and hurried down to the edge of the lake. The rabbit wasn't that far out but too far for him to reach it. He noticed Zoey running round the lake a little way to grab the orange lifebuoy ring, which was probably a better idea than him crossing the ice to get the rabbit. Although he wasn't that good an aim – he was probably more likely to kill the rabbit by hitting it over the head with the lifebuoy than save it.

The rabbit had clearly seen them and was heading further into the lake to get away from them. The ice definitely looked thinner in the middle than it did at the edges.

Kit swore under his breath and started stripping down to his boxer shorts.

'What are you doing?' Zoey said as she returned with the lifebuoy.

'I don't think that's going to help, not unless your aim is spot on and mine definitely isn't. Look at how heavy that lifebuoy is, we might squash it.'

'Why are you getting undressed?' Her voice was unnaturally high.

As he turned to look at her he realised she was staring at him appreciatively. She quickly shifted her gaze away but that made him smile.

'If I go through the ice, at least I'll have something warm and dry to put on after.'

'If you go through the ice, you might get trapped under the ice and die.'

'I think it's unlikely the lake is that deep, at least not near the edge.' He pulled his boots back on and dragged gloves from his jacket pockets and put them on too. God it was so cold.

'Jesus, Kit, be careful,' Zoey said. 'My first aid skills are probably as good as yours.'

He took a deep breath. What the hell was he doing, risking his life for a bloody rabbit? He got down on all fours and crawled out carefully onto the ice. To his relief, the ice took his weight.

'No looking at my ass,' Kit said, as he gingerly moved

out towards the rabbit and he heard Zoey stifle a giggle behind him.

'Here, take my jacket with you,' she said, sliding her coat onto the ice next to him. 'You can throw it over the rabbit when you get there, otherwise you won't be able to bring him back.'

'Good idea.'

He shuffled forward, sliding the coat along the ice as he moved forward. The rabbit wasn't moving that quickly, its little body flat on the ice as its paws frantically skidded across the slippery surface.

Suddenly the ice cracked beneath Kit and he froze.

'Oh god Kit, just leave it, it will probably find its own way back to shore. I don't want you to die saving a rabbit.'

He was shivering so much now but the rabbit wasn't that far away. He eased himself forward slowly and although he could hear the ice shifting beneath him, it didn't give way. He moved forward a few more metres. The rabbit was getting more and more frantic the closer he got. He picked up the jacket and threw it over the animal. The rabbit stilled underneath the coat for a second or two before the frantic movements resumed.

Kit crawled forward and carefully scooped up the creature inside the jacket, holding it close to his chest. It made a few desperate attempts to escape but, when it realised it couldn't, it went very still, though Kit could feel its heart beating furiously against his hand.

It was slow-going now he only had one hand on the ice as he shuffled and crawled back to the shore. And although the ice made plenty of noise as he passed over the top of it, it didn't break.

Finally he made it back to shore and put the coat down on the ground, carefully lifting the fabric away from the rabbit. As soon as the rabbit was free, it shot off like a rocket without so much as a backward glance.

'Well, that's gratitude for you,' Kit said, getting up and rubbing life back into his knees.

Zoey passed him his coat. 'Here, put this on and let's go back to my cottage, you can get dressed and warm up.'

He nodded, his hands shaking as he pulled on his coat. His skin was painfully cold.

'Getting undressed seems a bit foolish now,' Kit said.

'So does risking your life to save a rabbit,' Zoey said, rubbing his shoulders. 'Come on.'

She took his hand and started running back towards her cottage. She opened the door, flicked on the lights and ushered him inside.

'Get dressed and I'll get a fire going,' Zoey said, turning her attention to the logs in the fireplace.

He pulled on his jeans, t-shirt and jumper but he still felt so cold.

Soon golden flames were flickering in the fireplace and Zoey stood up and assessed him.

'Sit down,' she said and he did as he was told, still shivering. She wrapped a blanket around him. 'I'll make some hot chocolate.'

She walked off to the kitchen and he heard her moving around. Slowly warmth returned to his body, seeping through his bones.

She came back carrying two mugs of hot chocolate, passing him one. He wrapped his hands around it. To his surprise, she lifted the blanket and cuddled up next to him.

He watched her in confusion and she saw him looking at her.

'Body heat, don't get any ideas.'

'Of course not.' He shifted the mug into one hand and then tentatively wrapped an arm around her shoulders, holding her closer. She didn't seem to mind. 'Body heat is a very good idea.'

She smiled and slid an arm around his stomach and waist, resting her head on his chest. It felt divine and she smelt amazing.

He turned his attention to his hot chocolate in an attempt to distract himself from her wonderful proximity. He took a long drink. It was deliciously creamy but there was also a subtle kick of Christmas spices, cinnamon, nutmeg and other wonderful flavours.

She let out a little giggle.

'What?'

'For as long as I live, I will always remember you crawling across the ice in just your boxer shorts.'

Kit groaned. 'They're not even my best pair. I'm not making the best first impression on you, am I?'

She smiled. 'You just risked your life to save a rabbit, you're doing great.'

He frowned slightly. 'What about all the other stuff?'

'The fact that you're kind, funny, selfless, easy to talk to? Yeah, you're such an awful person.'

He stared at her, her beautiful green eyes locked on his. He swallowed, his heart filling with hope. For the first time since Lily had left he suddenly really wanted to take a chance with another relationship. Zoey made him want to be brave. With the log fire crackling, her cuddled up next to him on the sofa, staring at him as if he was some kind of hero, it would be so easy to get carried away. He could lean down and kiss her and then make a complete fool of himself if she still wanted nothing more than friendship.

He took another swig of his hot chocolate for fortification and then cleared his throat. But before he had a chance to say what was on his mind, to kiss her or ask her out, Zoey spoke instead.

'I think you were right about what you said before,' she said.

He racked his brains for what she meant. What had he said before?

'When you said the real relationships, the ones that work, are built on really strong friendships. I think that's so true. So I think I'd really like to be friends with you, Kit Lewis.'

He stared at her, a myriad of emotions crashing through him. Disappointment mostly mixed with a tiny bit of relief that he wasn't going to put his heart on the line after all. But the way she was staring at him made him think she wanted something more.

'I really like you, and if we were to have a proper chance at having a relationship I think we need to be friends first. What do you think?' she said.

He swallowed, his heart suddenly thundering against his chest as he understood what she meant.

'I can think of nothing I'd like more,' he said quietly. 'I'd really like to be friends too.'

He'd never uttered those words to a woman before but he meant them. This felt like it would be the start of something wonderful.

She smiled in relief.

He stuck his hand out for her to shake and she took it, her warmth filling him as they touched.

A large smile filled her face and he knew he probably had exactly the same smile on his face right now.

He finished his hot chocolate and placed the mug on the coffee table next to him.

'I should probably go.'

'Stay a while, make sure you're warmed up properly. I don't want you getting hypothermia.'

'No, that wouldn't be good.' He rested his head on the back of the sofa and closed his eyes for a moment. 'Tell you what, you let me know when you think I'm sufficiently warm enough.'

She snuggled in closer. 'Oh, I will.'

He smiled to himself as he felt his body relax into the sofa. He'd come to Jewel Island as a bit of a distraction from the memories of his last disastrous Christmas, to make a bit of pocket money selling churros and to spend time with his sister with no expectations beyond that. He certainly hadn't got his hopes up it would be anything wonderful. Despite the odds, he got the impression that this Christmas was going to be a really good one.

CHAPTER 3

18 DECEMBER

Zoey woke when the muted wintry light from outside filled the room. She opened her eyes to see she was still cuddled up to Kit on the sofa, her head resting on his chest, his arm wrapped around her shoulders. They'd spent the night together. So much for just being friends.

She didn't move for a few moments as she stared at Kit while he slept. He had long, dark eyelashes that cast gentle shadows across his cheeks. His full lips were parted slightly. His jaw and throat were covered in a dusting of stubble. He looked sexy.

He had this wonderful cinnamon aroma and she wasn't sure if that was because of spending his day making churros and crêpes or whether that scent was his. She resisted the urge to press her face to his throat and breathe in his delicious smell. He was bound to wake up and then there'd be the awkwardness of being in such close proximity as if they'd spent the night together far more intimately.

Zoey carefully untangled herself from his embrace and stood up. He didn't even stir.

She went upstairs, showered and dressed and came back down to find that Kit was busy making breakfast in her little kitchen. He flashed her a grin as she walked into the room and then turned his attention back to flipping a pancake. It should have felt weird having him here in her space. She'd been on her own for the last ten months and she'd got used to it. She enjoyed the solitude, the peace and quiet. But it didn't feel weird, in fact it felt very right. She had an overwhelming urge to slide her arms around him and give him a big hug but she wasn't sure if that was appropriate either.

Although Kit soon resolved that. Happy that his pancakes were cooking OK, he wrapped his arm round her shoulders and squeezed her against him.

'Good morning,' he said.

She slid her arms around him, hugging him back. She frowned slightly at how completely natural this felt when she'd known Kit for less than twenty-four hours. She really bloody liked this man and that scared her a little.

He tilted her chin up so he could see her face. 'Is this too soon, me staying the night, cooking you breakfast, giving you a hug?'

'I was just thinking how nice it was to have you here. And when I came into the kitchen and saw you cooking breakfast I just wanted to hug you but wasn't sure if that would be weird.'

'And is it?'

'Not at all.'

He smiled and turned his attention back to the

pancakes. 'I've chopped some bananas, I'm not sure if you have some maple syrup,' Kit said, relinquishing his hold on her and dishing up the pancakes onto two plates.

'I do,' Zoey said, retrieving a bottle from the cupboard and placing it on the little dining table.

'I made coffee too,' he said, reaching over and grabbing... a teapot?

'In a teapot?'

'You only had instant coffee, which is not ideal when you're making breakfast. Ideally we'd have a cafetiere. I had to improvise.'

They sat down to eat and Zoey couldn't help giggle when he poured her a coffee from the teapot.

'These pancakes are really nice,' she said, tucking into hers.

'Thank you. I enjoy making them so it's no bother.'

'Well, I could certainly get used to having this for breakfast. Although I think I'd have to do a bit more running to make up for it.'

'You run?'

'Yes, although probably not as much as I should. From around April to November I go wild swimming in lakes and rivers but when it gets too cold I take up running instead. I can't say I enjoy it as much as swimming so I probably don't do it as often, but I like to go a few times a week. Do you run?'

She suddenly had a rose-tinted idea of them running together.

'Yes, but probably even less than you. I row. Me and my brother, Adam, are in a two-man skull team. That's those really long narrow boats. We're not very good though. I do it on my own too on a kayak.'

That explained why he had such muscular arms. He had strong legs and muscles in his back too. She'd had a good look at his body the night before when he'd rescued the rabbit. It was a sight to behold.

She shook her head to try to clear it of that wonderful image.

'So, I was thinking, as we're now friends, I'd like to help you get back your love for Christmas,' Zoey said.

He seemed to force a smile as he took a bite of his pancake. 'You don't need to worry about me. I'm not going to stamp on your Christmas spirit. And I'm OK, I get to spend Christmas Day with my new friend.'

'Well, we can do Christmas activities together. There's a carol concert today, although one with a twist, and there are several other Christmas events over the next few days – making gingerbread houses, icing cookies. I think there's some kind of snowball fight too,' Zoey said, hoping to entice him, but judging by his face she'd picked the wrong events to tempt him.

'Now that sounds very wholesome.'

'Come on, I'm trying to help.'

'I don't need any help, I'm fine as I am,' Kit said, his tone belying his words.

She cocked her head as she thought. 'Is there something more to your anti Christmas spirit than what you've told me? I get missing your parents and Christmas not being the same without them but, if Christmas was so important to them, I think they'd hate for you to be hiding away from it just because they aren't around any more. But this feels more than that. When we spoke about it last night, there was a bit of an edge to how you said it was a lot of fuss for one day.'

He frowned slightly for a moment and she knew she'd hit the nail on the head, there was something more going on here. But she wasn't sure he was going to tell her, nor was it her place to push him.

She reached out and took his hand. 'It's OK. Don't tell me if you don't want to. We don't have to do Christmassy things either if this is too painful for you.'

He shook his head. 'No, it's nothing like that and I don't mind talking about it, we all have ghosts of relationships past to deal with. I'm divorced. Got engaged two years ago, on Christmas Eve actually. I'd planned this big romantic proposal because I wanted Christmas to be a special time for us. We got married four months later, in April last year, and my wife asked me for a divorce eight months later on Christmas Day.'

Her heart fell. 'Oh crap, Kit, that's terrible timing. What a way to ruin Christmas.'

He nodded. 'It had been so long since I'd celebrated Christmas properly and I thought with Lily we could make our own Christmas traditions. I tried so hard to make it special but ultimately our whole relationship was a complete sham. She was cheating on me the whole time we were together, before we got engaged and throughout our short-lived marriage. And not even with the same person, there were several people she slept with while we were together.'

'I'm sorry.' Zoey knew what that felt like, the betrayal, the belief that she wasn't enough. 'I think it's harder when you're married. You've made those vows to each other, that commitment for life, and for your wife to throw all that away after such a short time must have been devastating.'

'It was. I thought what I'd had with Lily was forever but looking back now it was clear we didn't really have much in common. She must have known that though before we got married for her to be cheating on me even before we walked down the aisle. She went ahead with the wedding anyway, keeping her secrets. Was it too much to ask for complete honesty in a relationship?' He looked at her and shook his head. 'I probably shouldn't be telling you this as it paints me in a bad light.'

'Wait a minute, this doesn't paint you in a bad light, not at all. It paints her in a bad light, but her infidelity is her issue, not yours.'

'You don't think that she cheated because of me?'

'I think she never realised how incredibly lucky she was to have someone as wonderful as you in her life.'

He stared at her and cleared his throat, turning his attention back to his breakfast for a moment.

'Well, anyway. I look back to me proposing to her on Christmas Eve and how supposedly excited she was and it was all fake. It had to be. There's no way she ever really loved me if she could be unfaithful throughout our whole marriage. And I suppose all of Christmas feels fake, when you think about it. People try too hard to be happy and excited about the big day. They put on elaborate dinners for friends and family because that's the done thing at Christmas, when really they get stressed out about it all and end up having arguments with their guests. People give to charity at Christmas because it's the season of goodwill, but not at any other time of year. I don't know, I just feel cynical about it all.'

'Oh Kit, I'm sorry. But I don't think it's Christmas you really have an issue with, I think it's just that your ex-wife ruined Christmas for you. You wanted to create your own Christmas traditions with her because Christmas has always been special for you and you wanted that again. If she asked for a divorce in the summer would you hate that time of year instead?'

His mouth twitched into a small smile. 'Fair point.'

'I think you're right that some people put unnecessary pressure on themselves over Christmas to have the best dinner or the best party but you can have a simple celebration without the need to impress anyone. What was it you wanted for your own Christmas traditions?'

'I didn't really have anything set in stone. I suggested to Lily that we go ice skating on Christmas Eve but she didn't want to do that. I thought I'd cook her a nice meal, we'd watch a movie and then open one present from each other. Although she wasn't a fan of Christmas movies so we didn't do that either. And also she didn't want to do the present thing because she'd never bother wrapping them until last thing on Christmas Eve. But those were my ideas for Christmas, I was open to suggestions. I'd hoped we'd come up with some traditions of our own but I don't think she was big on Christmas either.'

'OK, we could do those things,' Zoey said. 'As friends. We could give a present to each other on Christmas Eve. Have a meal together and watch a movie. There's a Christmas wreath-making workshop this afternoon and tonight we could go ice skating. Tomorrow night, how about we make mince pies here and then we can decorate a tree afterwards? We can get a small one from the market and buy some ornaments and decorate it together, just like you did as a child. I know it won't be the same without your parents but you don't have to reserve those kinds of things for your memories, we can do them again, make them our memories too.'

'OK,' he said, tentatively. 'That does sound fun and, in the interests of friendship, I'd be happy to do these things with you.'

She couldn't help the smile spreading across her face.

'Good. Now we better get a shift on. The market opens soon and I don't want to be late.'

Zoey was having a good morning in terms of sales. She'd sold one original and two prints and four mugs so far; maybe the added Christmassy elements were appealing. People came to the markets to look for unique things for Christmas gifts so maybe more customers would be willing to take a chance on her quirky paintings. Marika had been having a steady stream of customers all morning, enjoying her gingerbread biscuits and joulutorttu, so Zoey had definitely benefitted from such a high volume of customers next door.

It was a quiet lull right now so she looked around her shop. She was proud of what she'd achieved over the years, refining her style until it was something that was uniquely hers. As a child she'd started her painting journey with flowers, whole meadows of brightly coloured blooms, but her mum's friend, Mike, had been busy painting village scenes and so she had started to copy him. He had been delighted that she was inspired by him and spent a long time teaching her the basics. He had a quirky style to his paintings, charming, wonky houses, big curly waves and lots of bright colours. Mike had been quite famous in his time, everyone knew his name, or rather the name he painted under, Jack Ashley. He even had his own little TV show, *Painting with Jack*, which had been oddly popular on BBC2. People would tune in to watch him paint because he had this wonderful calm manner and they loved watching his paintings come alive. He'd also do little segments during which he gave hints and tips too. People loved him for his quirky artwork and for his warm personality and he was no different off-camera either.

Zoey had done her own versions of his work when she was younger and Mike had loved them. After he'd died she had developed her own style. She had started adding comedy to her paintings too: a dog stealing some sausages, a woman's bikini top floating away from her, a seagull stealing an ice cream, or a bag of chips. People seemed to like them.

She wondered what Mike would make of her work now. She looked at the two paintings at the back of the shop in the gold frames which were his and which she had no interest in ever selling. Two wonderful village scenes which she loved especially because the flowers at the bottom of the pictures were hers. When he'd suggested a collaboration whereby she would do the flowers she loved to paint so much on his picture, it had been a wonderful sign of his support for her. Nobody knew of her contribution and she loved that little secret. Those paintings hung in his world-famous gallery alongside all his other works of art and every day people from all over the world would come to admire the paintings. Before he'd died of cancer he'd taken these paintings down from his gallery and given them to her. She'd treasured them ever since.

These two paintings had been the last two he'd done before he'd had a stroke and after that the artwork in his gallery had changed a bit. It was similar to his previous stuff but it was never quite the same. Most people were very gracious – they loved a Jack Ashley painting no matter what. They still sold well, which was the important thing. But some people were critical; the innocent charm was *too* childlike, Jack had lost his shine. Zoey had felt so bad for him. He'd been very laid-back about it all but it had to have hurt.

She suddenly heard a strange deep vibrating noise from next door which carried on for a really long time and had different tones. She peered round the corner into Marika's shop and smiled when she saw Marika sitting down playing a didgeridoo. She really liked Marika and she was quickly learning to expect the unexpected with her. Zoey stood there watching her for a moment; the music was quite beautiful in this deep, earthy tone.

Zoey realised she wasn't the only person watching Marika. Elias, the Finnish man who was selling the way-too-hot glögi, was standing just outside Marika's hut and he looked absolutely mesmerised by the music... or Marika.

Suddenly Marika noticed him and stopped playing, blushing slightly. Elias stepped forward and started talking to her. Even though Zoey couldn't understand a word of what was said as they were speaking in Finnish, it was quite clear from the body language that they were busy flirting with each other. Although strangely, it seemed the topic of conversation was about Marika's didgeridoo, which was a weird thing to talk about if you were flirting. But then who was she to judge? Kit had thrown a bucket of water over her as his opening gambit and she knew she was already hooked.

Zoey turned away, giving them some privacy, and made Marika's peppermint tea just as she liked it. As Elias left, she poked her head around Marika's entrance.

'Hey, how's it going?' Zoey said, offering out Marika's drink.

'Thank you.'

Marika seemed a bit flustered as she took a sip.

'I think Elias likes you,' Zoey said and smiled when she watched Marika blush.

'I'm not sure, he was picking on me about my didgeridoo.'

'What's wrong with your didgeridoo?' Zoey said.

'He said I should be playing something more Finnish like the kantele.'

'What's a kantele?'

'It's the national instrument of Finland, you pluck the strings.' Marika gestured by plucking some imaginary strings on the table in front of her.

'Like a harp?'

'Sort of. But it's a solid piece of wood. It makes a very different sound to the harp. Personally I don't like it.'

'There's nothing wrong with you playing the didgeridoo,' Zoey said. 'But I think he was just using that as an excuse to talk to you, it was quite obvious he was flirting with you.'

Marika touched her hair self-consciously. 'Do you think so?'

'I do. You could tell.'

Marika thought about it for a moment and then dismissed it with a wave of her hand. 'Never mind about me and Elias, what about you and Kit? I saw you two together last night when I was leaving and later when I went out for a walk I saw you walking back towards the hotel holding hands.'

Zoey couldn't help the grin from spreading across her face. 'I really like him, Marika.'

'I can tell.'

'We just click in a way I've never felt before. I feel really excited about where this is going. We've agreed to be friends right now. We've both had relationship disasters in the past year so I think we're both a bit cautious about starting something with someone new, but we want to spend time getting to know each other, so, who knows what might happen.'

In reality, she was half regretting the offer of friendship. Kit made her want to throw caution to the wind and embrace the attraction between them. She wanted to go out on a date with him and kiss him and see if the chemistry that seemed to bubble between them was something real and tangible. She felt like this was going to be something special between them and she wanted to get to know him on that level now not later. But developing a friendship was probably a good starting point for anything more serious.

She glanced round and saw Lyra and Nix heading her way. They were the events managers up at the hotel and the ones responsible for arranging the Christmas market. She'd met them a few times now, while the market was being built and she was setting up her own hut. Apart from being lovely, they were also a couple, newly engaged. Zoey wondered what it was like to work alongside the man you were going to spend the rest of your life with. There'd been times when she'd been engaged to David that he'd irritated her beyond belief. Thankfully, he had his work and she had hers so they weren't in each other's pockets. She couldn't have imagined twenty-four hours a day with him, and that was when she'd been happily planning the wedding. It would have to be someone very special to want that kind of twenty-four-hour arrangement.

Zoey waved goodbye to Marika and ducked back inside her own hut.

'Hey, how's it all going?' Nix said.

'Good. I've done a few of these kinds of markets before, but I never really saw how they could be profitable, once you'd paid for your pitch. But I'm doing really well here. I'm not sure if it's just because everyone is in the Christmas spirit or whether my Christmassy-themed village scenes are more popular but I've sold a lot already. I'll certainly be doing more of these in the future.'

'Well we were thinking we might hold something like this in the summer,' Lyra said. 'It's been a big success.'

'Oh well, I'd definitely come back for it if you did, with summer-themed pictures this time.'

'That's good, we'd be happy to have you back.' Lyra cleared her throat awkwardly. 'We just wanted to pop down and have a chat with you. We, erm… saw what happened yesterday.'

Zoey was confused for a second and then felt her face flame red. 'You saw me rip my top off in front of the whole market?'

Nix looked awkward. 'Umm, the thing is, thousands of people saw it. We have a webcam live streaming parts of the market so people can see what's happening here and come along. We're recording it too so we can use clips for advertising. When we suddenly got hundreds of comments where before we were only getting a handful, we looked back on the video and saw what had happened.'

'Oh my god,' Zoey said. 'I'm so sorry. I don't normally go around flashing strangers. It was the glögi, it was scalding hot.'

'Yes, we've had a few complaints about that already and we've spoken to Elias and he promised to make sure it was cooler today. He's using new equipment he hasn't used before and I think he's finding it tricky to get used to. Please don't apologise.'

'But now your market will be remembered for the flasher rather than for the wonderful stalls.'

'Please don't worry about that,' Nix said. 'Any publicity is good publicity for us but I'm afraid to say that because of, umm… your exposure, and Kit's reaction to you getting burned, the clip has kind of gone a bit viral.'

Zoey stared at them in shock. She cleared her throat. 'How viral?'

'Well, you know how these things can get copied and

shared so it's hard to know how many clips are out there. But the one we saw this morning had been viewed three and half million times,' Lyra said.

'Three and a half million people have seen my boobs?' Zoey squeaked.

She'd come away with the hope of keeping her head down while her ex-fiancé married someone else. The thought of David seeing this video and laughing at her with Vicky was enough to make her go cold.

'Well, the only saving grace is that you were far enough away from the camera that it's very hard to recognise you,' Nix said. 'I mean, we can see what happened very clearly, but all you can really tell from the video is that it was a woman with dark hair.'

'You knew it was me though,' Zoey said.

'Only because of your owl jumper, I'd seen you wearing it yesterday so I knew it was you,' Lyra said. 'And Kit is recognisable because we see him running out of his hut with the bucket of water. I really don't think anyone else would be able to tell who you are.'

That was a small relief.

'You better show me the clip so I know what I'm dealing with,' Zoey said.

Nix fished his phone out of his pocket, swiped his finger across the screen a few times and then turned it around for Zoey to see.

She spotted herself straightaway, walking through the market with her hands wrapped around the glögi. She saw the moment the boys bashed into her and then a few seconds later she watched herself yank her jumper off so

55

she was standing there in her bra. Not even her best one at that.

But it wasn't that that would have made the video go viral – people were walking around in front of her so you couldn't get a good view – it was what happened next: Kit running out with a bucket of water and throwing it all over her. If this hadn't been her in the video she would have laughed too. She looked like a drowned rat. And it was such an overreaction by Kit that she couldn't help smiling at it.

But Lyra and Nix were right, you couldn't really tell it was her. Her dignity remained intact. Well, sort of.

'I suppose it isn't that bad.'

'No, I don't think it is,' Nix said. 'We just thought you should know.'

'You know, a lot of the comments were wanting to know what happened between you and Kit next, especially with the way he drags you off to his hut,' Lyra said, just as an elderly lady walked past wearing a silvery white cloak.

'Oh, I saw the video too,' the lady said, coming to a stop and appraising Zoey. 'I thought the way your young man handled it was very heroic… and masterful.'

'This is Sylvia O'Hare, one of our regular guests,' Lyra said. 'She's also a romance writer and sees love stories where sometimes there isn't one.'

'I don't know, she got us pretty much sussed,' Nix said. 'Even when we were at the stage of not particularly liking each other.'

Lyra smiled. 'That's true.'

'Don't tell me you didn't fall head over heels for that young man after he saved you,' Sylvia said to Zoey.

'No, I… he threw a bucket of water over me, that isn't the normal way two people meet,' Zoey said, defensively.

'It's memorable, I'll give you that,' Sylvia said. 'Something you two will always look back on when you're older.'

'He gave me a t-shirt with snowmen in different sex positions,' Zoey said.

'Well, that shows he's adventurous in the bedroom,' Sylvia said, practically. 'We all need a bit of excitement in that department. Have you seen him since?'

'Umm, one or two times,' Zoey said, awkwardly.

'Have you seen him naked?' Sylvia asked. Clearly this woman had no boundaries.

But the question made Zoey blush because she had seen Kit half naked and enjoyed it, but not for the reasons Sylvia was thinking. Somehow Zoey didn't think Sylvia would believe that Kit had been rescuing a rabbit from a frozen lake at the time.

But the blush was all Sylvia needed for confirmation.

She chuckled. 'Well, it seems that his heroics did impress you after all.'

'Maybe if we spin this as some kind of romance story we could make this better,' Lyra suggested.

Zoey felt her eyes widen. 'I think the fact I'm fairly anonymous in the video is the thing that doesn't make this too bad. I'm not coming out as the woman in the video just to give these people some more ammunition.'

'No, you're probably right,' Lyra said. 'So what did happen next? I'm not sure I'd be too happy about having a bucket of water thrown over me.'

'Kit's lovely, it's hard to be angry at him. But there's

57

nothing to tell. He gave me a spare t-shirt and some free churros to apologise. That's it.'

She certainly didn't want to go into any details of them spending the evening together and their plan for his Christmas rehabilitation.

'Oh, and just so I don't expose myself again, where exactly are the cameras?' Zoey said.

'There's three, one down your row, one down Kit's and one at the entrance,' Nix said.

'Good to know,' Zoey said.

'Well, I think that live feed might make interesting viewing over the next few days,' Sylvia said, waggling her eyebrows.

'We'll let you get on, we have a few other people we need to see,' Lyra said.

'Why, did they expose themselves and accidentally made themselves a viral superstar too?'

Lyra laughed. 'Fortunately we only have one viral superstar to contend with now, but we thought we'd better go and inform Kit as well.'

Zoey winced and hoped that he would be discreet too. She certainly didn't want to add fuel to the fire.

They walked off and, after a few moments, Sylvia gave her a theatrical wink and walked off too.

It seemed she had already added fuel to the fire with that one.

CHAPTER 4

Kit couldn't help smiling as he stirred the churro mixture. What a difference a day made. It had been twenty-four hours since Zoey had entered his life in the most spectacular way and he couldn't be happier. Before her, he hadn't wanted to get involved in another relationship but Zoey had changed that. And although he was more than happy being just friends with her, right now he was excited by the possibility of something more.

He also found himself looking forward to Christmas for the first time in a long time. He wanted to do all the Christmassy things with her, like ice skating or making mince pies. He felt happy and nothing could burst his bubble.

'Craig has been in touch again,' Lindsey said.

Except that.

Kit sighed. His uncle Craig and his dad had had a big falling-out a year before his dad died. Kit knew Craig had spent most of his life with a gambling problem, losing thousands of pounds he quite simply didn't have. He'd even lost his wife because of it. He'd borrowed money from loan sharks with no way to ever pay them back. Which was where Kit's dad had come into it, bailing him out of one bad debt after another. Until, one day, his dad had simply refused. They hadn't spoken since and Craig hadn't even bothered coming to his dad's funeral. But since then Craig had got back in touch several times in an attempt to extend the olive branch, which Kit and his siblings hadn't been interested in accepting. Loyalty to his dad had stopped Kit from wanting to have anything to do with him because his dad had always refused to.

'You know he'll just want money,' Kit said. 'This isn't because he wants a lovely family reunion.'

'That's what I thought but he says he has something important to tell us about Dad, something he feels we should know.'

'Which is?'

'He won't say unless he can meet with us.'

'Another stupid trick just to get our attention.'

'I know but aren't you at least a little bit curious what he is going to say?' Lindsey said. 'Dad spent more time in London in his later years. Did you ever wonder why?'

'No, I just accepted that he was working down there. I guarantee there is no big secret here, it's just Craig using this as an excuse to meet so he can try and get some money out of us.'

'Maybe we should meet with him, see what he has to say,' Lindsey said, eyeing Kit to see his reaction. 'Him and Dad were always falling out while we were growing up, and they'd soon make it up again. Who knows, if Dad hadn't died shortly after they'd had that big row, maybe they would have been best friends again a few months down the road. It's unlikely they'd still not be speaking after all this time. Maybe Dad wouldn't want us to carry on his grudge on his behalf.'

Kit thought about this. 'I don't think they were ever best friends. They seemed to tolerate each other more than anything, but you're right that Dad seemed to forgive him fairly quickly. Sometimes it would be a few months before they'd speak again, but it was never years. Maybe we should at least hear him out.'

'I think too much time has passed for us to ever be close again,' Lindsey said. 'But beyond me, you and Adam, he's the only family we have left.'

He sighed. 'OK, see if he wants to meet up after Christmas. Unless he wants to come down here before the big day. We could do dinner at the hotel or one of the restaurants in the village.'

She nodded. 'I'll email him, see what he wants to do.'

Just then Nix and Lyra arrived. He'd met them a few times when he'd been setting up his hut. They seemed nice people.

'Kit, can we have a word?' Lyra said.

He frowned. That didn't sound good.

Zoey's phone rang later that afternoon and she knew almost immediately it would be Lulu, her best friend. They'd gone to school together, got their first Saturday jobs together and lived together. Zoey had been chief bridesmaid at her wedding and Lulu would have been the same at her wedding to David, despite Lulu hating him from the second they'd met. If anyone was going to recognise Zoey in that viral video it would be Lulu.

Zoey answered the phone.

'What have you been up to, Zoey Flynn?' Lulu asked by way of a greeting.

'I don't know what you mean?'

'I thought you were going to Jewel Island for a quiet holiday, instead you whip your boobs out at the earliest opportunity and go viral at the same time.'

Zoey laughed. 'How did you know it was me?'

'Because I knitted that jumper for you three years ago. I would recognise it anywhere.'

She'd forgotten that. Lulu loved her knitting machine and was always knocking out jumpers and clothes for friends. Zoey was grateful that it was only her jumper that was recognisable, not her.

'We get sent these viral videos all the time at work and we feature some of the best ones on our website. Imagine my surprise when one pops into my email starring my own best friend.'

Lulu worked on one of those popular magazines that featured fashion, celebrities, TV, films and clearly the odd viral video too. Zoey cringed at the thought of her video being shared with the millions of readers who enjoyed that magazine.

'It wasn't really my fault, it was the scalding hot mulled wine.'

'I'm more interested in the gorgeous man that came to your rescue.'

'The video is very blurry; how can you possibly tell that he's gorgeous?'

'Is he?'

Zoey laughed. 'Yes.'

'See, I know. And you and he are…'

'Friends… Currently.'

'Ha, I knew it,' Lulu said, triumphantly. 'You fancy him.'

'Lulu, I'm twenty-nine, not twelve. I'm… attracted to him.'

'Call it whatever you want, you still want to play hide the sausage with him.'

Zoey laughed. 'Oh my god, you are the worst. There's more to a relationship than—'

'Shagging them against the wall of the hut?'

'Than sex. I like Kit, I really like him, so we've agreed to be friends first.'

'You've always been all-or-nothing. Most people go on a few dates first, see if the chemistry is there, they don't start seeing someone thinking this is going to be marriage and forever, that kind of thing can come later.'

'I know, I know. I've always looked for serious relationships rather than something casual. I can't imagine going to bed with someone I didn't feel that deep connection with.'

'You have to kiss a lot of frogs to find your prince and sometimes those frogs can be a hell of a lot of fun.'

Zoey smiled. 'I know. I rushed into my relationship with David and look at how that turned out.'

'That's because you accepted a proposal from a man you barely knew. If you had just dated him with no expectations of anything more than a bit of a fun, you would have discovered he was a dick long before you got to that stage. It doesn't have to be a serious relationship with Kit, you can just see how it goes. How disappointed would you feel if you stayed friends for the next few months and then when you did kiss him or go to bed with him you have zero chemistry or he kisses like a tumble dryer? Best to find out that kind of thing now.'

Zoey rolled her eyes with a smile. 'You're married now, three beautiful children, so at some point your attitude of let's keep everything fun and casual must have changed.'

'I'm not saying I'm against marriage or serious relationships, I'm just saying you don't have to look for that from the beginning. Eric was a one-night stand but he was so good in that department I wanted a second night and a third until eventually we were seeing each other every night and I didn't want anyone else but him, but that took time.'

Zoey sighed as she rearranged some of her paintings in their stands. 'I think we just look at things very differently. I want the fairytale, I'm not going to settle for some guy who is sleeping with several other women behind my back.'

'Those silly romance books you read have a lot to answer for,' Lulu grumbled.

'Can we change the subject? You do you, and I'll do me, and we'll agree to disagree on how *I* should live *my* life. I'm thinking of moving here.'

'What? I know you haven't been totally happy in Copper Tree since you and David broke up, but I thought you might move back to London.'

'No, I don't think that was ever an option. When I moved to Copper Tree I fell in love with that small-town life, the friendly people and that community spirit, and I just never really felt that in London. And I've done London life, I grew up there. I've done the endless tube journeys and the packed buses, I've done travelling with my face in someone's armpit, I've done the nightclubs and bars where you need a small mortgage for a night out. I like the quieter, simpler life.'

'But I miss you,' Lulu said.

'I miss you too, but village life swallowed me up and I can't see I'd ever be happy living in a big city again. Besides, you know my dream has always been to live in a house by the sea. I feel like I could be really happy here.'

'Then I wholeheartedly support this decision. Follow your dreams. And if your dream is marriage and children with your gorgeous Kit, then I support that too. However you end up there.'

Zoey smiled. 'One step at a time.'

The hotel had organised lots of little Christmas events leading up to the big day but the one Zoey was most looking forward to was the big band carol service. She'd already seen musicians walking past heading for the bandstand with trombones, tubas, saxophones and trumpets. She'd even seen two people carrying a piano. They were going to play Christmas songs and carols but with their own unique big band twist.

She locked up her hut and, as Marika was doing the same, they walked the short distance to the bandstand at the end of their row together. She didn't think they'd lose out on a ton of custom by listening to the big band for half an hour. Almost all of the customers to the market were now standing around the bandstand waiting to hear the music too.

The band were busy tuning their instruments and getting their music sheets ready. Behind the bandstand a giant Christmas tree towered over the proceedings, the fairy lights twinkling.

'This is wonderful,' Marika said. 'I've seen big bands play a few times, but they normally play movie theme tunes or popular songs we all know. I'm looking forward to them playing carols.'

'It'll be something new for me too,' Zoey said.

'I might see if I can find Elias,' Marika said, subtly nodding behind Zoey.

Zoey looked over her shoulder to see Kit, hovering behind her. She smiled and turned back to Marika. 'You don't need to go.'

Marika laughed. 'And I don't need to stay and play the third wheel either.'

'There's no third wheel, me and Kit are friends just like me and you.'

'Definitely not like me and you,' Marika said. 'You two are the kinds of friends that want to see each other naked, preferably horizontal.'

Zoey laughed.

'You said you wanted to get to know each other so go and get to know him. Enjoy the music and you can catch me up when we get back to our huts.'

Marika disappeared into the crowds before Zoey had a chance to protest further.

Kit approached, his hands in his pockets. 'Sorry, I didn't mean to scare Marika away.'

'I think she's trying to give us some space. I didn't think a carol concert would be your thing.'

'I'm open to my re-education. Especially when I have such a lovely teacher.'

She smiled. 'Have you heard about our moment of fame?'

He cringed. 'Yes, I think your moment of fame far outshines my moment.'

'I wouldn't undersell your involvement in this.'

'Yeah, I'm sorry, I certainly made the video more… entertaining than it needed to be.'

'Judging by the comments they all think you're some kind of hero,' Zoey said.

He smiled at this. 'I don't think anyone has ever thought I was heroic before.'

'Well they do now. Lots of people are hoping that some kind of romance will come of it.'

'That would be crazy,' Kit said. 'Who would agree to go on a date with someone who threw a bucket of water over them?'

'It depends if the person who did the throwing is pretty bloody special, then I think all transgressions would be forgiven.'

He smiled and moved closer. He swept a hair from her face. 'I'm not sure what I did to deserve that forgiveness but I'm so damned grateful for it.'

She swallowed because there was something wonderfully intimate about that gesture. It wasn't exactly something a friend would do but she found she didn't care.

'It was the spectacular churros that did it.'

'I'll remember that for next time.'

'Next time you throw a bucket of water over me?'

He laughed. 'Next time I do anything to upset you, I'll bring churros.'

'Good plan.'

Seamus, the village mayor, came onto the bandstand and switched on the microphone.

'Thank you all for coming,' Seamus said. 'I'm very excited to welcome the Penzance Big Band who are going to perform some Christmas songs and carols for us today. So let's give them a big Jewel Island welcome.'

Seamus broke out into loud applause and everyone in the crowd joined in too.

The band launched into a big dramatic instrumental version of 'I Wish It Could Be Christmas Every Day' which had everyone clapping and dancing along.

'Do you wish it could be Christmas every day?' Zoey teased.

Kit laughed. 'Maybe not every day.'

The band started playing 'Jingle Bells next'; it was very upbeat and over the top, which was clearly what they did best.

Although Zoey was finding it hard to concentrate as Kit stood next to her, shoulder to shoulder. She could feel his warmth, smell his Christmassy scent. Standing this close to him made her heart race.

Their hands were back to back, almost touching, but as the songs continued Kit brushed his hand gently against the back of hers and then, ever so slowly, he looped one finger round hers. She couldn't help smiling as she let her fingers entwine with his. It felt so right. She got the feeling she was going to be really bad at being just friends with him.

The performance was energetic, vibrant and completely different to any carol concert she'd ever been to and when it came to an end everyone burst into applause.

Zoey turned to Kit. 'Well, what did you think of the carol concert?'

'It was good, I enjoyed it.'

'Really?'

Kit laughed. 'Really, I'm not a total grinch.'

'Well as you're in the festive spirit, shall we go and buy our tree now? Then we can do the wreath-making workshop they are running all afternoon. Or do you need to get back to making churros?'

'I've closed the hut for an hour or two as Lindsey has a dentist appointment so I'm all yours.'

'I think we better go and choose our tree first,' Zoey said. 'Maybe we should buy something fairly small.'

'I think we should buy something big,' Kit said, relinking his hand with hers as they made their way to the small Christmas tree lot at the end of the market.

Zoey laughed. 'It's a small cottage and if we buy a huge tree we'll have to buy lots of ornaments to fill it. Not to mention we'd have to transport the thing all the way up to Moonstone Lake.'

'Well actually the Christmas tree seller delivers the trees to anyone on the island,' Kit said.

'Damn it.'

'But I do take your point about buying lots of ornaments to fill it. How about something medium sized?'

'OK, I have to say, you're a lot more enthusiastic about the tree than I thought you would be,' Zoey said.

'I think I'm reliving my youth, I'm really looking forward to it.'

Tiny snowflakes started falling, swirling and fluttering in a gentle breeze, and with the golden glow of the fairy lights strewn across the huts it looked magical.

'There's still so much of this market I haven't seen yet,' Zoey said. 'I need to have a proper wander round to appreciate all the different huts. Look at that one with the snow globes. I love snow globes. Some of them are so intricate. I always fancied getting a snow globe of every place I've visited, but I never remember until I get home.'

'We can have a look now, see if they have any of the countries you've been to.'

'I'm not sure it's the same thing, buying them in retrospect. I think if I bought a New York one now, it would always remind me of the Jewel Island Christmas market where I bought it rather than of New York.'

Kit nodded. 'Fair point.'

'I also don't think I want a New York one. As much as I loved the city, I went there with David, my ex-fiancé, and I think it would remind me of him.'

'Hey, if I'm not allowed to hate Christmas because of my ex then you can't hate New York because of your ex.'

Zoey laughed. 'That's fair. And I could never hate New York. Maybe I need to go there with someone else, create new memories just like we are doing for you and Christmas.'

She looked at him and he grinned.

'I've always wanted to go,' Kit said.

'Well, maybe we can go together,' Zoey said, delighting in the image of the two of them exploring the city together.

'As friends?' Kit clarified.

She laughed. 'As friends. New York does Christmas very well, it can be a continuation of your rehabilitation.'

'I'm sold. So what's the deal with your ex? Is he someone I need to beat up for you?'

Zoey laughed. 'He's very big.'

'Is he someone I need to have a stern word with?'

She laughed loudly. 'That's OK, I've already had a lot of stern words with him. He was the complete cliché. Ten months ago, I walked in on him sleeping with his assistant in our bed.'

'Oh shit.'

'You haven't heard the worst yet. Our wedding was all planned for this Christmas Eve – the venue, the menu choices, the flowers, the bridesmaids' dresses – and instead of cancelling the wedding he just swapped my name for hers. Everything else they kept the same. I'm not even bothered he's marrying someone else two years after he proposed to me, they're welcome to each other, but it's weird, right?'

'Very. I wonder how she feels about taking your wedding day, that the venue, the menus, all of that was yours.'

'Oh, I think Vicky is desperate to marry David. If he'd told her he wanted to marry her jumping out of a plane stark naked, she'd have done it. He's quite wealthy. And before you ask, no, that wasn't why I was marrying him. It was one of those whirlwind love affair things, I had no idea how rich he was when we first met. Looking back now, I have no idea what I saw in him. We never took the time to really get to know each other. That's why I want to make sure we're friends first – if we do end up together, we'd have more of a solid base to build from. I know a lot of people would just go out on a few dates and see how it goes but I get the feeling that with us it would be something serious very quickly.'

'I think so too and I'm happy to take our time to get it right.'

She stared at him. So many men would run a mile if a woman talked about a serious relationship after just one day but she knew they had a rare and wonderful connection.

They reached the Christmas tree lot where there were trees of all shapes and sizes. Different shades of green too, from the deepest bottle green to the brightest grass green and every shade in between. Some of the trees had been sprayed with glitter or fake snow and some were just beautiful in their natural simplicity.

'What kind of tree should we get?' Zoey asked. Who knew there were so many different types?

'I don't know, but it has to look, smell and feel right,' Kit said, running his fingers gently over one of the nearby branches. Whatever he felt obviously didn't meet with his approval as he moved on to another tree.

Zoey sniffed one and then another and surprisingly they did smell different. 'I think we had Scots pine trees for my wedding to David.'

'Then we won't be getting one of those.'

'Why not? We were told it was a good one.'

'Because we certainly don't need any reminders of that

cretin or the wedding that got stolen from you.'

'How do you know he was a cretin?' Zoey said. 'I mean, he totally was but you never met him.'

'I don't need to. He was unfaithful to you, the man was an idiot. If we were together, I'd never want to let you go.'

'Oh, you don't know me yet, I could have terrible disgusting habits that make you run away or skeletons in cupboards.'

'They'd have to be really bad habits.'

'What counts as bad?' Zoey asked. 'What's a dealbreaker for you? What's important in a relationship?'

Kit had clearly been teasing her but now his face grew serious. 'I think the one thing I'd always want in a relationship is honesty. If there is a problem, we'd talk about it, not keep it buried. No secrets.'

'I agree. I think if a relationship isn't working you have to be honest with each other before it becomes damaged beyond repair. And I don't agree with secrets either, they just lead to distrust and lies.'

Except there was a big secret Zoey had kept to herself for the last fifteen years. It was something she would most likely take to her grave but it would never have any impact on Kit; he didn't need to know about it. He wasn't talking about that kind of secret anyway. He just wanted to know that if they did get together, he'd never come home one day and find her in bed with another man, and she could categorically promise that would never happen.

'Then at least we're on the same page with regards to that,' Kit said. 'How about this one?'

Zoey sniffed the tree. 'It doesn't smell of anything.'

Kit sniffed it too and nodded. 'You're right, it doesn't

have any kind of scent.'

'What about this one?' she said, pointing to one with needles that had a hint of silvery white about them. It was the perfect shape and not too big or too small.

They both bent their heads at the same time to sniff it and almost headbutted each other.

Zoey laughed and stepped back. 'You first.'

Kit bent his head again and took a sniff. He smiled. 'It smells of Christmas.'

Zoey took a sniff too and sure enough it did, kind of dark and spicy. 'I think it's perfect.'

She signalled to the owner and he came over and tagged the tree, writing the address of where they wanted it delivered on the tag.

'Cash or card?' the man said, producing a card reader.

'Oh, card please,' Zoey said, grabbing her purse from her bag.

'Let me pay,' Kit said.

'No, it's my cottage, my idea, I'm paying,' Zoey said, pushing her card into the reader before Kit could object.

'But this is for my benefit, I should pay,' he said.

'But I want to do this for you, we're friends, I can do nice things for you,' she said and then turned back to the man. 'We wanted to do the Christmas wreath workshop too, has that started yet?'

'Yes, my wife is running it over there,' the man said, handing her a receipt. 'Go and join her.'

Zoey turned to Kit. 'Come on, I think we'll be good at this.'

❋

Kit followed Zoey to the group of long trestle tables where there were a collection of people all trying their hands at making their own Christmas wreaths. There was a woman in a red apron directing the proceedings.

The woman came over to greet them.

'We'd like to make a wreath please,' Zoey said with the complete confidence of someone who knew their wreath was going to be amazing.

Kit wondered if being an artist gave her that creativity and skill in other areas too.

'Sure,' the woman said. 'I'm Imogen, and I'll show you what you need to do. Are you wanting to do one each or together?'

'Together,' Kit said.

Zoey looked at him. 'You don't want to do one each? We can compete, see who can do the best one.'

'My fingers are definitely not green. I have killed plants in the past just by looking at them.'

'You don't have to have any gardening skills to be able to do a wreath,' Imogen assured them. 'It's very easy.'

'Still, I'd rather work together, many hands make light work and all that,' Kit said.

Zoey shrugged. 'That's fine by me.'

'So here is your wire frame,' Imogen said, handing them a circular wire about two inches thick. 'And over here I've cut a selection of different foliage to approximately the right length. You can choose what you want from there. Basically you are looking to make several small bouquets like this.'

Imogen collected three bits of foliage – a small sprig of holly, some ivy and some ferns – and then quickly wrapped the stalks together with wire to make a small bouquet.

'You'll probably need around twenty of these. Then you attach them with more wire so the bouquet is sideways on the wire frame like this and work your way around the circle with the bunches overlapping until it is completely covered.'

Kit watched her quickly attach the small bouquet to the ring and then just as efficiently add another and could instantly see how this would look when it was finished. It did actually look a lot easier than he'd first thought.

'We also have a few baubles, berries and ribbons you can add afterwards for a bit of colour. I'll be hovering around here, so give me a wave if you have any problems or questions,' Imogen said as she hurried off to help a nearby family with their wreath.

Zoey started picking up some sprigs of holly, poinsettias, ivy and ferns and Kit collected some gold-painted pine cones and a few fake sprigs of mistletoe because he thought the white berries would look good with the red flowers. They sat down together.

Zoey seemed quite adept at handling the sprigs of foliage. Kit started tying some of the sprigs together into small bunches and instantly cut his palm on the wire.

'Ouch!' he said, sucking the side of his hand where blood started to appear.

'Oh no, what did you do?' Zoey said, dropping her sprigs.

'It's nothing, just a little cut.' He showed her and blood appeared around the wound again.

'Doctor! We need a doctor!' Zoey called out and Kit

laughed.

Zoey rummaged in her handbag and pulled out a packet of wet wipes. 'Here, let me take a look.'

She took his hand in hers and the warmth and softness of her skin against his was something wonderful. She carefully wiped the cut.

'Does that hurt?' She looked up, her eyes locking with his. His heart leapt in his chest as she continued to watch him, her fingers gently stroking across his palm.

He shook his head. 'Not one bit.'

Imogen came hurrying over, breaking the moment. Zoey let go of his hand, clearing her throat.

'Oh no, did you hurt yourself?' Imogen said. 'It's this new wire I've been using. I couldn't get hold of my normal stuff so I bought this and it's really good except that it's so sharp. I've cut myself a few times on it already. Here, put a plaster on it.'

She rummaged in the pockets in the front of her apron and pulled one out. Zoey took it, peeled it open and placed it gently over the cut.

Kit exchanged a look with Imogen and she smiled. 'Well I can see you're in safe hands.'

Imogen moved away as Zoey smoothed the plaster over his skin. 'I think you'll live.'

'I think so too.'

She let go of his hand and turned her attention back to the wreath and he watched her for a moment, picking out the different sprigs of foliage.

'Do you have a garden back in your home?' Kit said as he resumed tying the bunches, with a little more care this time.

'No, I never have. I grew up in a few different flats in London. Even when I moved in with my best friends when I was twenty, we lived in a small flat then, but it had a small balcony so I was able to at least have a few potted plants. When I moved in with David he lived in this large house but the only outside space we had he'd filled with a swimming pool and a hot tub so I didn't have one then either. I always wanted a nice garden, where I could spend my time growing roses, lupins, trailing a clematis over the walls. I always wanted a dog too, but couldn't because of the lack of a garden. Maybe if I moved here, I could finally have one. What about you – not a keen gardener then?'

'It wasn't something I was ever interested in when I was growing up. Mum loved it but I remember it being a lot of work and I was always too busy with my little doodles to want to spend time with seedlings and pruning roses. The house overlooking the harbour that you spoke about before, that has a garden, doesn't it?'

She nodded. 'A large one.'

'Have you been to look at it yet?' Kit asked.

She shook her head, focusing on attaching one of the small bunches to the wire frame.

'Why not? Can you afford it?'

'Yes, actually, and I have some money in savings too.'

'So what's stopping you?'

Zoey attached some berries to the frame and for a while she didn't speak. 'It has always been my dream to live in a little cottage with a garden overlooking the sea. It was my mum's dream too but she always said it was a retirement dream and now she is living it. I suppose for me the reality of dreams doesn't live up to the hype.'

78

She grabbed a pine cone and attached that too, before she continued.

'When I was growing up, me and my two best friends, Lulu and Florence, always said we'd get a place together one day. We talked about it a lot, planned where it would be and what it would look like, and finally when we did I was so excited to be living the dream. But the reality of that was living in a tiny flat with a view of a brick wall, listening to Lulu shagging her boyfriend every single night and arguing with the two of them over whose turn it was to empty the bin and who had drunk the most milk or whose fault it was we had a hundred-pound phone bill. We don't even speak to Florence any more after one stupid row which caused her to move out. After spending my child-hood reading fairytales and my teenage years reading romance stories, I always envisaged that the cherry on top in my life would be getting married, raising a family, but the reality of that was getting engaged to a man I barely knew only to have him cheat on me in my own bed. My dreams have been a bit disappointing. What if living in a cottage overlooking the sea doesn't live up to the dream either?'

'I don't think we should be afraid of following our dreams.'

'I know, but the reality is not always what we imagine it to be. My friend Florence was obsessed with a drummer in a local band when she was eighteen. She finally met him, slept with him and he was a complete dick. My friend Lulu works on one of those celebrity magazines and she has worked with or met a ton of celebrities – pop stars, actors, TV presenters – and she is always telling me eye-popping stories about the celebs, most of them turn out to be really disappointing. Plenty of us have celeb crushes but I think a lot of people are disappointed when they actually meet them. I wonder if the dream of living in a seaside cottage is better off staying a dream.'

Kit thought about that for a moment, while he tied a bunch of foliage to the frame so it overlapped the other bunches. 'I don't think that's true. Maybe the celeb crush thing is true, maybe for some people they are probably better off not knowing the truth, but meeting or not meeting a celebrity crush is not going to have any real impact on anyone's life. But living in a house by the sea would. And if you don't grab this opportunity now you'll always be wondering, what if? Besides, what's the worst that can happen? You end up with a house you don't actually like, you can move out and find another. It doesn't have to be forever.'

'That's true.'

'And what if someone else snaps it up, won't you be disappointed?'

'Well, yes.'

'And the Zoey I know, the woman who became a full-time artist, that takes guts to live that dream. It's not financially rewarding, you could have easily become an accountant or a bank manager, which would have paid much more than painting pictures for a living, but you didn't because painting was your passion. Shouldn't your dream of living in a house with a garden overlooking the sea be your passion too?'

She looked like she was considering this.

'Why don't we go and have a look at it once we've

finished making the world's best wreath,' Kit said, although in truth their wreath was looking more than a little sad.

'We could,' Zoey said, a slow smile tugging on her lips. 'OK, then, let's do it. Just a look though, no guarantees I'll take it.'

He nodded. 'It's at least worth a look.'

Suddenly the time and care that Zoey was taking on the wreath went out the window as they hurriedly tied a few more bunches to the frame and stuffed a few more berries and pine cones on the wreath too.

Imogen wandered over. 'How are you getting on?'

'I think we're pretty much done,' Zoey giggled. The wreath was nowhere near done.

'Oh,' Imogen said, trying to hide her disappointment. 'Maybe it needs a few more bunches here and, umm… and there,' she pointed to areas where the frame was very clearly still visible.

'We like the minimalist look,' Kit said, handing over the money for the wreath and the workshop. He grabbed the wreath in one hand and Zoey's hand in the other and quickly hurried away before Imogen could persuade them to add more berries or ribbons.

As it happened, Will, the estate agent, was on his way to visit his mum who lived two doors down from the cottage when they popped in to ask if they could view the property. And as the cottage was completely empty of furniture and valuables, he was quite happy to leave them to it while he went to see his mum.

Zoey stood on the balcony overlooking the sea and couldn't help the huge smile spread across her face. Kit had been quiet as they walked around and she knew he was trying to let her make her own mind up and not push her to take it if she didn't want it. The place needed a bit of TLC, and several rooms would be improved by a lick of paint. The garden was just a patch of grass and a few plants and it would take a lot of work to make it look beautiful and full of life again. Right now the cold wind was blowing right off the harbour and making the house rattle a little. Waves were crashing over the harbour walls and Zoey could feel the spray on her cheeks.

Kit came to join her on the balcony and shivered a little, pulling his coat around him tighter. They were completely exposed to the elements here; there was nothing between them and the sea, which was wild and dramatic in its current form.

'What do you think? I know it's cold out here in the winter but you have log burners on each floor, and central heating of course, so I think you'll be very cosy,' Kit said. She looked at him and he held his hands up. 'If it's not right for you, don't take it, there'll be other houses.'

'Kit, I love it. I can imagine myself here painting my pictures, cuddled up by that fire in the winter, sitting on the balcony in the summer, tending to the roses in my garden, playing with my dog. I can picture it all so clearly.'

Zoey didn't want to say that she could also imagine him there too, feet up on the sofa, reading a book, their dog curled up by his side. That was definitely jumping too far ahead when they were supposed to be just friends.

'How we getting on?' Will appeared behind them. 'The

old owners retired to Spain and weren't sure whether to rent or sell. They couldn't face the house being on sale for months and having to do loads of improvements to get it ready for market so I recommended renting. You'd have free rein to do what you like with the place and in a few months, if you were happy here, I'm sure the owners would be very happy to sell it to you.'

Kit gave her an encouraging nod and she turned to face Will.

'I'll take it,' Zoey said.

Kit was waiting for Zoey outside the ice rink. He'd left her to go back to the estate agents to fill in all the forms as he needed to get back and sell some churros and crêpes, but they'd agreed to meet after the market had closed to go ice skating as part of making his own Christmas traditions and his rehabilitation.

He was so pleased Zoey had taken the house of her dreams, he was excited for her to move here. He just had to find his own slice of happiness now, because living in the same house he'd shared with his wife was certainly not causing him any joy. Maybe he could find a place somewhere nearby, on the mainland perhaps, as there didn't seem to be many houses available on Jewel Island. He felt like he wanted to pursue this friendship with Zoey once Christmas was over and not just let it fade away because they were no longer in the same place together. Even if nothing ever came of it, now she was in his life, she was too important to let go.

His phone rang in his pocket and he fished it out, noticing it was his brother.

'Hey Adam, how's it going?'

'Good. The kids are bouncing off the walls with the excitement of Christmas but we're all good. Lindsey tells me you've got yourself a girlfriend.'

Kit rolled his eyes. Adam was such a patronising twat. He made it sound like Zoey was his first ever girlfriend and Kit was thirteen years old again. And Lindsey had clearly been stirring up trouble, telling Adam what he'd been up to.

'I've met a woman who is nice and we're friends. There's nothing more to it than that. Don't tell me you rang just to give me a hard time about that.'

'I'm not giving you a hard time, it's great you're finally getting back out there after what happened with Lily. I never liked her and you've been too afraid to move on after what she did for fear of getting hurt again. This friendship is definitely a good thing. Tell me about her.'

Kit sighed. 'Her name is Zoey and…'

Where could he even start with describing her? She was wonderful and he knew he could fall for her so easily.

'… And I really like her,' he said, softly, and then cringed, waiting for the piss taking that was sure to come.

'Then go for it, ask her out. What are you waiting for?'

'She's been hurt in the past too, she's made it very clear she just wants to be friends right now and I respect that.'

'Then show her how brilliant you are. Woo her without her knowing.'

'She has to be ready to move on too, I'm not going to push her on this. Besides, I like being friends with her, there's no pressure to get it right and we can really get to know each other before we do take that step.'

Adam was silent for a moment. 'You know, me and Eshana were friends for years before we started dating. We've been happily married for six years next month. Maybe there is a lot to be said for friendship.'

Kit smiled. Adam and Eshana were as solid as a rock. If he had something half as strong as what they had, he'd be very happy.

'Anyway, I didn't really ring you about your love life, as interesting as that is. What do you think about all this Craig stuff? Lindsey said you're going to meet with him,' Adam said.

'I honestly don't think anything good will come from this,' Kit said.

'I don't think so either. He sent me a friend request last year on Facebook and in a drunken moment of naivety I accepted. He sent me a message and, within two minutes of polite chit-chat, he was asking to borrow some money. Apparently he owed someone some money and he *had* to pay them back by the weekend or there would be consequences. Of course there were the fake promises that he'd pay me back when he got paid from work, just like he used to say to Dad, despite him telling me he wasn't working right then. I quickly unfriended him after that. I can see he's moved on to Lindsey now, maybe he thinks she'll be a soft touch.'

'You never told me this,' Kit said.

'I didn't think much of it to be honest, just Craig up to his old money-grabbing tricks. I haven't heard from him for eighteen months or more so I'd kind of put him out of my head. But now he wants to meet up with you two, makes me think he's just after money again.'

'I bet it's that. He's told Lindsey he has something important he wants to tell us about Dad, but I think it's just a ploy so we'll agree to meet with him and then once he has us there he'll feed us some sob story about needing some money,' Kit said.

'What could he possibly have to tell us about Dad? It's been nearly ten years since he died. If he really has something to tell us, and it's something bad, I'm not sure I want to know. I have wonderful memories of Dad, I don't want them to be tainted now.'

'You'd rather live in blissful ignorance?'

'Yes exactly,' Adam said. 'My rose-tinted world is a nice place to live.'

Kit smiled. He wasn't sure he shared that sentiment but he understood it.

'Lindsey wants to meet him, so I'm obviously going to go with her. But I have zero expectations for this so my hopes can't be dashed. I'll let you know how it goes.'

'OK and let me know how it goes with your lovely Zoey too.'

Kit grinned. 'I will.'

He hung up the phone just as Zoey came up. She was practically bouncing with excitement. He couldn't help smiling at her. God, he liked her so damned much.

'Hey, you ready to go ice skating?' Zoey said.

'I am. I'm not sure if I'll be any good though. I used to go skating when I was a kid but that was a very long time ago.'

'Well, ice skating seems to be a very Christmassy thing

to do so it's perfect for your rehabilitation,' Zoey said.

They paid and then exchanged their shoes for skates. They stepped on the ice. Thankfully Zoey seemed to know how to skate because, as romantic as it would have been to hold her hand and teach her how to do it, he felt a bit rusty himself and wasn't confident in his hand-holding abilities, at least not when skating. Although to his surprise, after a bit of a wobbly start, it all came back to him and it seemed it really was like riding a bike, you never forgot.

'I can't believe I've got a house overlooking the sea,' Zoey said, a huge smile on her face. 'I mean, I have to wait for my references to be approved and I've got to pay the deposit, but Will reckons I could move in at the start of January. This is honestly a dream come true and you made that happen.'

Kit shook his head. 'No, it was your decision. You had to take that step. I just gave you a tiny little nudge. And I'm so pleased that it's worked out for you. I think it will be a bit of work at first getting it how you want it but totally worth it. And I'm always happy to give you a hand.'

'Bath is a bit far to pop round for half hour of painting,' Zoey said.

'Maybe I'll move closer.'

She looked up at him in surprise. Moving house to be closer to a friend he'd just met was clearly too much too soon.

'I like the idea of living near the coast too,' he added. 'I've pretty much lived in and around Bath all my life, I definitely feel the need for change. I'm not talking about pitching up on your doorstep. Just somewhere coastal.'

'I wouldn't mind if you did, I think we'd make good

87

neighbours. But of course I'd force you to decorate the outside of your house with an abundance of lights every Christmas.'

He smiled. 'I'd be OK with that.'

She grinned and looked up at the sky for a moment as she skated along next to him. 'The stars are so clear down here, it's so beautiful.'

He watched her, her face lighting up with a smile. 'Yeah it is. Very beautiful.'

A kid pushing one of those penguins to help him skate suddenly came to an abrupt stop right in front of him and Kit quickly manoeuvred round the child so as not to crash into him.

'Ooh, fancy moves,' Zoey said, grabbing hold of the side to avoid crashing into the kid too. 'When you said you used to skate as a child, did you mean for fun or…?'

'Oh no, figure skating. While other boys were playing football I was learning the toe loop, the Salchow and the triple axel. My forward glide was particularly impressive.'

They carried on skating round the rink.

'That's amazing, what happened? Why did you give up?'

'I realised girls preferred footballers to figure skaters.'

Zoey laughed. 'Nooo! You gave up your dream to impress the girls?'

'It was never my dream. I enjoyed doing it, but I'd gone as high as I could go without entering competitions and I was never in it to prove I was the best or to compete at some national level, I just did it for fun.'

'Come on then, show me your stuff,' Zoey said, excitedly.

'Oh hell no. It's been around twenty years since I last

skated, I've forgotten most of it. I mean, the basics of skating are still there, but I couldn't do any jumps. Besides, the rink is too busy, I'd probably land on some unsuspecting child. And I'm not really the showing-off kind of man.'

'Just do something small,' Zoey pleaded.

'I could skate backwards,' Kit said, flipping on the spot and skating next to her going backwards, but there really were too many children around to do that for any length of time. He turned back to face the right way.

'That's so good. I can barely skate properly in the right direction, let alone backwards. Do you have anything else you could do, that impressive forward glide maybe?'

Kit laughed. 'I could probably stretch to that.'

He picked up speed a little then leaned forward, bringing one leg out behind him. His hips were certainly not as flexible as they had been when he was nine years old, but for a few seconds the glide was nearly perfect.

Until he stumbled and landed flat on his face, his chin grazing painfully across the freezing ice.

'Oh my god, Kit, are you OK?' Zoey asked, kneeling down next to him and then falling on her bum. She burst out laughing.

'Yes, I'm fine, but my pride is definitely dented.' Kit sat up and rubbed his chin. It was sore but it didn't seem like it was bleeding. He clambered to his feet and then helped Zoey to her feet too.

She took his face in her hands and looked at him. 'I think that will be sore tomorrow.'

'It's sore now,' Kit said.

To his surprise, she leaned up and placed a gentle kiss

right over the graze. 'Is that better?'

Christ, how did he answer that? Her soft kiss had sent his heart racing, his chin tingling with her touch. Part of him wanted to say no so she'd do it again.

He nodded and she smiled.

'When I was little, my mum used to give me magic kisses when I'd fall over and cut myself. They always used to make me feel better.'

Magic was definitely one word to describe how he was feeling right now. God, he wanted to lean down and kiss her properly. Except he'd promised her he was happy being friends. She wanted to take the time to get to know him properly, he couldn't just grab her and kiss her.

He cleared his throat. 'Thank you.'

She laughed, having no idea what was going through his head. 'Did you lie to me about your skating abilities to impress me?'

'No, I genuinely had skating lessons when I was a child. It was a long time ago though. I don't lie about stuff like that. I might not have had an impressive life, my ex-wife certainly wasn't impressed by me and I didn't have a serious relationship before her, but I'm not going to lie to make myself sound better. What you see is what you get.'

Zoey grinned. 'Good attitude. Don't ever change to please someone. Personally I think you're pretty damned perfect just the way you are. For what it's worth, I don't lie either.'

They started skating again.

'Ever?'

'Oh well, I suppose everyone tells small lies. How many boyfriends or husbands, when asked by their wives or girlfriends if their bum looks big, will answer a resounding no without even looking at it? I think little lies told for the right reasons are OK.'

'I think so too. If someone goes to the effort of spending hours making a dinner that tastes awful I'm not going to tell them. So what do you think is the biggest lie you've ever told?'

She was silent for a moment.

'Have you ever called in sick at work because you just couldn't be bothered or you were hungover?' Kit prompted.

'The biggest lie I've ever told was a big one. I was fifteen and it was done to protect someone I cared about. It was done for the right reasons and I don't regret it.'

'Now you have me intrigued,' Kit said.

Zoey laughed. 'And it's something I can never tell anyone so I'm afraid that will have to remain a mystery.'

'What?' he laughed. 'You can't tell me something like that and then not divulge the details. Can you not tell me anything?'

'It wasn't really my lie, it was someone else's, so I really can't share any details about it, but I was the one who helped them to pull it off.'

'Now I'm imagining all kinds of scenarios,' Kit said.

'Well stop imagining,' Zoey said. 'In that regard I will have to remain a woman of mystery.'

'Were you a teenage spy?'

Zoey laughed. 'Yes, I was a trained assassin.' She did karate hands to prove it.

He took her hand to stop her waving them around like a mad thing. 'I'll take my chances.'

CHAPTER 5

19 DECEMBER

Zoey hurried along to Kit's hut the next day. They had arranged to meet at lunch so they could buy their tree ornaments for their big tree-decorating session that night.

She was relieved that Kit had dropped the subject of her big lie last night. She shouldn't have said anything at all but there was something about him that made her want to tell him every single thing about her. She felt like she could really talk to him about everything and there would never be any judgement. But her secret was not hers to tell and she needed to be more careful in the future.

Kit waved to her as she approached and, after a quick word with his sister, he came hurrying out to meet her.

'Come and say hello to Lindsey for a second before we go shopping, she's dying to meet you,' Kit said.

'Of course, I'd love to meet her,' Zoey said.

'Word of warning,' Kit said, quietly. 'Subtlety isn't her strong point.'

Zoey grinned. She'd had plenty of practice fending off Lulu's suggestions and inappropriate comments over the years so she was fairly confident she could cope with whatever his sister threw their way.

He ushered her over with his hand on her back. 'Zoey, this is my *lovely* sister Lindsey,' Kit said, somehow making the word lovely sound sarcastic and over the top at the same time. Lindsey returned his sarcasm with a quick fake grin and Zoey couldn't help smiling. She was an only child so didn't have that kind of sibling relationship whereby you hate your brother or sister but secretly love them at the same time. 'And this is my *friend* Zoey,' Kit said, making it very clear to his sister there was to be no inappropriate comments.

'Zoey, it's lovely to meet you,' Lindsey said, genuinely. 'This one has been talking about you non-stop for the last few days.'

Kit sighed softly next to her.

'He thinks you're pretty amazing,' Lindsey said. 'As a friend.'

Zoey smirked. 'I think he's pretty bloody brilliant too. As a friend.'

'So tell me, was it his idea to play Pictionary the other night?' Lindsey asked.

Zoey looked at him. 'It was actually.'

'Was this before or after he told you what he did for a living?'

'Oh, I knew before,' Zoey said.

'He normally keeps that quiet at games nights, then whips out Pictionary and thrashes everyone. It's his secret weapon. He's always been good at doodles and drawing, he used to do funny cartoons of the teachers at school – the other kids loved them, the teachers not so much.'

Zoey looked at Kit. 'I can't imagine you being a rebel at school.'

'That was pretty much as rebellious as he got, straight A student here, you've got yourself one of the good guys,' Lindsey said.

'Except I haven't really *got him* yet.'

'I meant as friends,' Lindsey said, with a smile. 'You've got yourself a really good *friend.* Sweet, funny, kind, he has it in spades. And according to some of his ex-girlfriends, he's pretty good in bed too.'

Zoey burst out laughing.

'OK, I don't think there's anything more embarrassing or quite frankly weirder than my sister talking about my sex life, so we'll cut this lovely greeting short,' Kit said, ushering Zoey away. 'I'll be back in about an hour and me and you can have a little chat about what's appropriate and what isn't when meeting my friends.'

'Look forward to it.' Lindsey waved at him sarcastically.

Zoey couldn't say for certain but she was pretty sure Kit also gave his sister the middle finger as they walked away, although Lindsey certainly didn't seem to mind.

'Sorry about her,' Kit said when they were far enough away.

'Don't worry, if my best friend Lulu was here you'd be getting the same treatment. She thinks I'm crazy to just stay friends with you. She thinks my all-or-nothing attitude is silly. She says we should date and have some fun rather than going for the full-blown commitment of having a relationship.'

'And what do you think about that?'

'I think...'

She honestly didn't know what to think any more. She was attracted to Kit in ways she'd never felt before. She really liked him and was definitely interested in being more than just friends. But her cautious heart wanted to take the time to get this right. She wanted what Kit's parents had, the everlasting bond, and that kind of love was worth waiting for.

'I think we should get a move on if we're going to buy all our ornaments in an hour.'

Kit smiled. 'OK.'

'Right, where should we go to get our ornaments?' Zoey said as they walked around the market. 'Are you more of a traditional or modern man when it comes to Christmas decorations?'

'I'm not sure. I normally have a little tree in my own house, with a few baubles on it. When I was a child, all the tree decorations were ones me, my brother and sister had made. Or special ones we'd bought on family holidays, ones that were based on that place, like the Eiffel Tower from our trip to Paris or the Statue of Liberty wearing a Santa hat from my parents' trip to New York. I don't have anything personal on my tree now.'

'Well, I think personal items are a good place to start, although we're not going to find the Eiffel Tower or Empire State Building here. We might find things to do with our hobbies, like rowing or painting.'

'Maybe we should buy ornaments for each other. I know we don't know each other that well, but we could buy things we think the other might like,' Kit suggested.

'OK, I love that idea. We should probably buy some traditional items too to fill out the tree, some baubles and fairy lights, but I like the idea of buying for the other person.'

'OK, shall we split up? Meet back here in half an hour?'

'Good idea.'

Kit set off in a run as if taking part in a race and she liked that he was taking this seriously.

So many of the huts were selling different tree decorations that it was hard to know where to start but she wanted to take her time to get it right. She bought some basics first, some warm white twinkly lights, gold pine cones and some creamy flowers with glittery petals just to fill out the tree a bit. She added a few gold baubles too.

She started looking around at some of the more modern decorations and ornaments, searching for something that would reflect Kit and his personality. She saw something that looked like a curly churro dipped in chocolate so she bought that. There was one hut that was selling everything farm-animal-themed, which was cute but not really relevant to Kit, and she was about to turn away when she saw a silvery bucket ornament which made her smile, as that was how they had first met. She didn't know enough about him or his life to be able to do this task justice, but she could buy things like the bucket and the churro that reminded her of him. She bought the bucket and a rabbit then walked to the stand next door and bought a Christmas pudding to represent the jumper. She found a red glittery pencil ornament which she thought symbolised his job. She also bought a Christmas tree ornament in honour of him learning to love the festive season again.

Soon it was time to meet Kit, so she headed back to

where she'd last seen him. He was already waiting for her, clutching a bag in his hand.

'I'm excited to see what you got for me,' Zoey said.

'I'm looking forward to seeing what you chose for me too, but I don't want to leave Lindsey on her own for too long so I better get back to the hut to sell the churros. We can share what we've bought tonight,' Kit said.

'Oh, sure, no problem. Why don't you come round to my cottage about six?'

'OK, sounds good,' Kit said, and then bent his head and kissed her on the cheek.

He immediately stepped back, frowning, but Zoey could still feel the touch of his lips against her skin.

'Sorry, that probably wasn't appropriate for our *just friends* arrangement,' he said.

Zoey swallowed. 'No it's OK, friends hug and kiss each other on the cheek.'

'OK,' he said, slowly. 'What about on the lips?'

She grinned. 'That's probably too friendly.'

'Right, and sex?'

She laughed loudly. 'I have never had sex with any of my friends before. I think that definitely falls into the box of being too friendly.'

He nodded, his mouth twitching in a smirk. 'Good to know.'

'There's a line,' Zoey said.

'Yes and I'd never want to cross it.'

She stepped closer to him, entwining her fingers with his again. 'I wouldn't say never.'

He smiled. 'I really better go, because if we stand here

97

any longer talking about *that* I'm never going to leave. See you tonight.'

'I look forward to it.'

She watched him go with a big smile on her face. Tonight was going to be fun.

CHAPTER 6

When Kit arrived at Moonstone Cottage later that night, he was surprised to see Zoey bundled up against the cold as she stood outside. Snow was gently falling all around her so it didn't seem the perfect time for her to be outside.

As he drew closer he realised she was drawing on her art pad, which was propped up on an easel.

'What are you doing? It's freezing out here,' Kit said as he got closer.

'The lake is so beautiful tonight with the snow, I had a sudden urge to paint it. I'm just sketching out a rough drawing now and I'm using these colouring pencils to try and take a note of the beautiful colours. I've taken some photos too.'

He moved round by her side to have a look. The sketch was very rough but he could see she had real talent.

'This is wonderful.'

'Oh, thanks, it's nowhere near finished yet. My style is normally quirky, filled with humour, but when I have something so magnificent right on my doorstep I just want to capture that simplistic beauty without making it silly or wonky. There, that will do for now. I'll paint it later.'

'Do you mind if I sketch my version of the lake too?' Kit said.

Zoey turned over the pad to a fresh page. 'Go ahead. I'll go and make us some hot chocolates to warm us up.'

She disappeared inside and he looked at the lake. It really was wonderful tonight. He drew a few simple features: stick trees, the lake, the snow blown in mounds on the banks. And then he added a few extras too.

Zoey came back out, passed him his chocolate and then burst out laughing. 'Oh my god, I love it.'

At the front of the picture he'd drawn the head of a terrified cartoon rabbit, staring right at them. And in the corner he'd added his famous Brian and Bert, the fox and badger, who were watching the rabbit as if it was insane.

'You've captured them brilliantly,' Zoey said. 'If they'd been there to see the rabbit on the lake the other night, they would have looked exactly like that. This is so good. I can't believe you knocked it out so quickly.'

'Oh, I know Brian and Bert like the back of my hand, I can draw them very easily. Normally I take my time with them, but this was just a quick sketch.'

'Can I have this?'

'Of course.'

'I will treasure it, thank you,' Zoey said.

'Can I have yours?'

She grinned. 'As soon as it's finished. Come on, let's go inside.'

She grabbed the pad and he picked up the easel and

they went inside Moonstone Cottage. The snow was falling quite heavily now and he shook it out of his hair.

Zoey took off her coat; she looked stunning in a pale blue dress with little Christmas trees all over it.

'You look lovely,' Kit said and kissed her on the cheek, which made her smile. He knew he was pushing the boundaries of what was acceptable in any normal friendship, but it didn't seem to bother her. In fact, it was very clear she liked it.

'Thank you, I thought I should dress appropriately for the occasion.'

He shrugged out of his coat and looked around the room. The log fire was burning happily in the fireplace, there were candles dotted around the room and lots of twinkling fairy lights too. And there was the tree, standing proud in the corner. Even without any decorations, it looked good.

'I thought we could decorate the tree first. I have a casserole in the oven so we can eat once we're done and then we can make some mince pies.'

'Sounds good,' Kit said.

'But first, let me show you the decorations I bought for you,' Zoey said, excitedly, grabbing a bag and bringing out several parcels wrapped in tissue paper.

He sat down on the sofa. 'Should I unwrap them in any particular order?'

'No, any order is fine,' Zoey said, sitting down next to him.

He unwrapped the first one and smiled when he saw the rabbit. She giggled; there was no explanation needed there. He opened up the bucket next, which was very appropriate, and then the Christmas tree.

'Because you love Christmas,' Zoey said.

He grinned, because with Zoey he felt like he could very easily fall in love with Christmas again. Her enthusiasm was infectious.

He opened up the Christmas pudding next.

'Is this for the jumper?' Kit asked.

She nodded. 'I'll treasure that jumper forever.'

He smiled and opened up an ornament that looked like a pencil, which he presumed was because of his job.

'I love these, thank you,' he said, opening up the last ornament. He stared at it. It was quite obvious it was a dog turd and he didn't know what to make of it. All the other ornaments were linked to how they had met or to parts of his life, like drawing. How was a dog turd representative of him? Was it just supposed to be a joke? That must be it, she was trying to be silly.

'Do you like it?' Zoey asked, obviously concerned by his silence.

'Sure, it's funny,' he forced a laugh. 'Thank you.'

He placed it down on the coffee table with the others. He supposed he was thankful that it would be hanging on a tree in her house, not his, so he wouldn't have to see it.

She cocked her head. 'Funny?'

Christ, if it wasn't supposed to be funny, then what did she mean by giving him a dog turd?

'Well, yes, poos are funny, I guess.'

Her eyes widened. 'Poo? That's not poo.'

'I'm pretty sure it's supposed to be dog poo.'

'No, it's a churro, dipped in chocolate.'

He burst out laughing, mainly in relief. 'Is that what it is?'

'You thought I'd bought you a dog poo ornament? Is that really a thing?'

'Oh, I'm sure it is. Don't forget we have poo emojis on our phones and now we have poo emoji cushions that we can cuddle up to,' Kit said.

'But who would want dog poo on their Christmas tree?'

'Pretty much any boy under the age of sixteen who thinks poos are funny.'

Zoey picked it up and looked at it. 'Oh my god, I've bought you a poo ornament.'

Kit couldn't stop laughing. 'And I'll treasure it forever.'

She laughed. 'Let's just discard that one, we don't need it.'

'Oh we do, it's going front and centre on the tree,' he said, standing up and hanging the poo in the middle of the tree.

'Nooo,' Zoey giggled, 'I can't have a poo on my tree.'

She moved to take it off the tree but he caught her hands to stop her. 'We'll tell anyone that asks that it's a churro.'

'But I'll know the truth. These things really should be labelled.'

'Like maternity jumpers?' Kit asked.

'Yes exactly.'

'How about I show you what I've bought you and we can forget about the dog poo ornament, at least for now.'

'OK, but I'm not sure how this will make me feel better, unless you've accidentally bought me something horrific too,' Zoey said.

'I think I'm fairly safe this time. But let's see,' Kit said.

He passed her the bag with the ornaments in and she started unwrapping them. The first one was an owl with large googly eyes wearing a Santa hat.

'This reminded me of your jumper, the ruined one,' Kit explained.

'It does look a lot like the owl from my jumper,' Zoey said, giving it a little shake to make the eyes jiggle. Then she frowned slightly. 'But you didn't see it, I'd ripped my jumper off before you got there.'

'Ah,' Kit said, rubbing the back of his neck awkwardly. 'Well, I was watching you before you spilt the mulled wine.'

'You were watching me? Why?'

He paused, trying to come up with a plausible answer that didn't sound creepy, but he had nothing. 'Because I thought you were beautiful.'

She stared at him. 'Oh.'

An awkward silence fell over them.

'Sorry. I know that's not something a friend would say but it's the truth.'

'No, it's OK. Don't apologise for it.'

He cleared his throat. 'Open the next one.'

She unwrapped an ornament of a glass of mulled wine. 'Oh this is cute.'

The next ornament she unwrapped was a mince pie.

She laughed. 'I'm not sure our pies are going to look this perfect tonight, but I think wonky pies are infinitely more tasty.'

'Agreed.'

The next ornament she pulled out of the bag was a cute

man and woman hugging, with their names written underneath.

'I thought we should have something to celebrate our new friendship arrangement,' Kit said.

She smiled as she ran her fingers over the two figures but she didn't say anything.

'They had a whole range, couples kissing, getting married, pregnant couples, couples with children or pets,' Kit went on.

'A whole life portrayed in the medium of tree ornaments,' Zoey said.

'Well, maybe it was a sign,' Kit teased and saw her eyes flicker with something he couldn't define.

'Maybe it is,' Zoey said, softly. She turned her attention back to the couple in her hand. 'I love it.'

'Well I have one more ornament for you.' He gestured for her to open the last one. He was fairly confident about this one at least.

She unwrapped the small snow globe and he heard her take a little breath.

'This one is a Jewel Island snow globe. I thought you should probably start your snow globe collection somewhere.'

'I think Jewel Island is an excellent place to start,' she said, quietly.

She stared at it for the longest time and he was just starting to think he'd made a mistake in buying it when she suddenly leaned over and hugged him.

He smiled and wrapped his arm around her.

'Thank you, I love it.' She quickly let him go and stood up. 'Come on then, let's decorate our tree.'

She busied herself getting out all the traditional decorations and baubles as if she suddenly realised it wasn't right to be hugging him but he didn't agree. It felt very right.

'I think the key to great mince pies is the pastry,' Zoey said as they surveyed the ingredients laid out on the kitchen worktops after they'd cleared away following dinner.

'And you think frozen roll-out pastry is the key to great pastry?' Kit said, doubtfully.

'Yes, because all the measuring and mixing has been done for us, by experts no less. So we can't go too far wrong. We don't even need to worry about getting the right thickness because that's been taken care of too.'

'But it's not been made fresh. This pastry was made by some machine probably months ago, you can't beat freshly made pastry to get that perfect mince pie.'

'OK, Mr Expert, why don't you be in charge of making the pastry and I'll be in charge of the mincemeat.'

'When you say in charge of the mincemeat, do you mean you'll be the one spooning it out of a jar?' Kit asked.

'Exactly. It's a very important job.'

He studied the ingredients for a moment. 'I can't make pastry.'

Zoey laughed. 'Then I don't think you can be judgemental over my roll-out stuff.'

'Ah but I can, my mum always used to make fresh pastry and she'd tell me making it from scratch was the only way to make it.'

'My mum would always tell me life's too short to spend

it making pastry when we can buy roll-out stuff that does it for us.'

Kit laughed. 'Fair point.'

'OK, then a challenge. You make mince pies with your homemade pastry and I'll make them with the roll-out pastry and then we'll do a blind taste test to see which pie is best. I'm sure Google will be able to help you with a recipe and a technique. Hell, I'm sure there's a YouTube video with some TV chef taking you through a step-by-step.'

Kit nodded. 'OK, you're on. Then you'll see what pastry perfection really tastes like.'

He spent a few minutes searching the internet on his phone while she undid the box and laid the sheet of pastry across the unit.

'Looks like I'm beating you already,' Zoey said.

'It's not a race, the winner will be the one with the best pie,' Kit said, measuring some flour into a bowl.

Zoey selected a large mug and a smaller one to cut out the pastry tops and bottoms and spent a few minutes doing that before lining the foil pie cases with the bottoms, filling them with mincemeat from the jar and then adding tops. She pressed the pie edges together and then turned to see how Kit was doing. His hands were in the bowl as he rubbed the fat into the flour. It was clear he knew exactly what he was doing.

'I think you've done this before.'

Kit grinned. 'A few times when I was a kid, although I couldn't remember the measurements. And it's been a long time since I've done this. I actually loved this part of the run-up to Christmas, making loads of Christmas foods in the kitchen with my mum. We'd make mince pies, ginger-bread biscuits and Christmas cake.'

'Did she teach you how to make churros?'

'Yes, and I loved that. It's something so simple and quick to make but very effective. I've always loved baking, I think because Mum loved it so much, and I always imagined when I have children of my own that I'd pass it on. Although my ex-wife laughed at me when I said that. I'm not sure whether it was the thought of me teaching my kids to cook or whether the thought of having kids with me was so unappealing. The man she was cheating on me with was a chainsaw carver, so maybe she thought cooking wasn't manly enough.'

'Then she's missing out, watching a man cook is very sexy.'

He stopped what he was doing and stared at her. 'Sexy?'

'Well, maybe sexy is the wrong word but—'

'Hey, don't take it back, I was enjoying that for a moment.'

'OK then. I love watching a man enjoy himself in the kitchen, being creative with recipes, making desserts, main courses, starters. I love food and if a man enjoys making it then that's definitely a good thing. Cooking is an art form, combining ingredients together to create something wonderful, and while I'm not particularly great at it, I have a lot of respect for someone who is.'

'I think I preferred sexy over you having respect for me,' Kit said.

'Oh, you're very sexy right now,' Zoey teased.

He grinned and returned his attention back to the pastry.

'Do you think you're more like your mum or your dad?' she asked as she watched him. 'Your mum was into cooking and your dad was into art, and you kind of do both.'

'My dad was a very talented artist, he'd paint the most wonderful village scenes and I was never any good at stuff like that. Being a cartoonist is more about exaggerating features – big eyes, droopy ears – than making it accurate, so I don't think I inherited his talent for real art, but I did inherit his love of drawing.'

'And did you always want to be a cartoonist?' Zoey asked as he rolled out his pastry. 'Or a chef?'

'Oh no, I wanted to be a rock star,' Kit said and she laughed. 'I had the electric guitar I'd drive my parents mad with, the leather jacket, I even dyed my hair blue one summer. My parents were very supportive, until I told them I wanted my tongue pierced. They put their foot down on that one, which I'm very grateful for now.'

'I love this insight into your youth, were you in a band?'

'Yes, me and couple of my mates would make music together in the garage. We thought we'd take over the world.'

She helped him line the pie cases with his pastry bottoms and then worked with him to fill each pie with some mincemeat.

'Were you any good?'

'God no, we were appalling. We didn't even know how to write our own songs but we used to do a lot of covers, badly. What about you, what was your dream?'

'Oh, when I was little I wanted to be a mermaid, but

there's not much room for career development in that profession.'

'No, probably not. And I feel like, don't take this the wrong way, but I'm not sure you have the right qualifications needed to pull that off.'

'No, sadly I didn't have a tail.'

'Or the ability to hold your breath underwater.'

'Oh no, if I was a mermaid, I'd have gills so I could breathe underwater.'

'Right, of course,' Kit said, seriously.

Zoey smiled at the way this conversation was going. She felt like with Kit she could talk about anything, even her childish dreams of being a mermaid.

'When I outgrew that dream, I decided I wanted to be a fighter jet pilot.'

'Now that's a big transition between mermaid and pilot,' he said, placing the tops on his pies and then brushing them with milk. He transferred both trays into the oven.

'It is a bit, I thought it would be exciting.'

'I'm sure being a fighter pilot would be very exciting. What happened to that dream?'

'Well, I was in the Air Cadets for a while and it was a whole lot of marching backwards and forwards and making sure our uniforms and shoes were in pristine condition. I'd spend hours polishing my shoes so you could see your face in them. We did do some flying in little two-seater planes, which was cool, but the marching and cleaning my uniform wasn't really up my street.'

'No, I can understand that. And then you found art?'

'I was inspired by my mum's friend. I never thought

about making painting my career but it was something I was good at and absolutely loved. I can't ever imagine doing something else now, not even being a mermaid.'

Kit smiled.

'You know, you're very easy to talk to,' Zoey said. 'That's a wonderful quality to have.'

'That and being sexy when I cook.'

She grinned. 'That too.'

Half hour later, the pies were cooked. Both sets of pies looked good but the quality was going to be tested by taste not appearance.

'OK, how are we going to do this?' Kit said.

Zoey selected the best-looking pie from each batch and sat them on the counter. 'I'm going to blindfold you and then feed you a mouthful of each and you can choose which one you prefer. Then you can do the same for me.'

She grabbed Kit's red scarf and wrapped it around his head, covering his eyes. 'Can you see me?'

'No, I can't see a thing,' he said.

Zoey cut the pies in half and straightaway she could see the difference in the pastry. Kit's looked better and more appetising than hers. She touched the inside to make sure it wasn't too hot but it was safe to eat. She took a spoonful of hers and held it up for Kit.

'Here comes the first one,' Zoey said.

He opened his mouth and she carefully placed the spoon inside. He chewed on the pie thoughtfully for a minute.

'OK, next.'

'No judgement on that one?'

'I'll reserve judgement until the end.'

She smiled and gave him a spoonful of his. His judgement was much quicker this time.

'That's the winner.'

'Damn it,' Zoey said. 'OK, my turn.'

Kit whipped off his scarf and tied it round her head, plunging her into darkness. She heard him scoop up the pie and then he gently cupped her face with one hand as he fed her the spoonful with the other. He gently placed the spoon on her tongue and she sucked the mixture off.

Christ, there was something really intimate about the way he was feeding her and she didn't know why. But it suddenly felt like things had escalated beyond two friends trying mince pies to something more. Had he felt the same when she had fed him?

She played for time while she chewed, hoping he hadn't noticed her cheeks going red. But despite having removed the spoon, he was still holding her face.

She swallowed the piece of pie, no longer tasting it as every single sense was attuned to him. His smell, his warmth, his touch.

He cleared his throat. 'Ready for the next spoonful?'

She nodded. After a moment he fed her another mouthful and then ran his thumb just below her lip to wipe up a small drop of juice. She let out a little breath and hoped he hadn't noticed. She had made the rule about just being friends and now all she could think of was what it would be like to have him use his lips to remove that drop instead of his thumb.

She pulled off the scarf and looked at him. His eyes were dark with need. Christ, he'd felt that connection too.

'Which one was best?' Kit asked, his voice rough.

She had no clue. 'Umm, the first.'

He stared at her and then looked away at the pies. 'Well that was mine, so two–nil, I'm afraid.'

Right then she couldn't care less about the stupid pies. It suddenly felt like she had a choice to make. Either she could forget being friends and try dating him instead, but that felt like it could be a bad decision considering how quickly she had fallen into a relationship with David and how badly that had turned out. Or she could put some distance between her and Kit, which she really didn't want to do. As all she could think of right now was getting Kit to lick mince pies off other parts of her body it was quite clear they couldn't stay just friends.

Zoey sat on the sofa next to Kit, a mug of hot chocolate in her hands as she stared at their tree. She'd had the most wonderful night, decorating the tree with Kit, eating dinner and making mince pies. There was something so comfortable about talking with him, as if they'd known each other for years. He made her laugh too. But there was something much more than that that was happening between them, at least for her. When he touched her, when he kissed her cheek, it made her heart race. She wanted him to kiss her properly. The chemistry between them crackled in the air.

The ornaments he had bought her for the tree had meant something to her, especially the cute couple and the snow globe. She liked that the couple represented their friendship. The couple looked so smiley and happy and she thought that being with Kit was going to make her very happy. She knew it was silly, but she wanted to add all the others in that range of ornaments to her collection too. She loved that he'd bought the snow globe for her because she said how much she liked them and a Jewel Island one to remind her of her time here. No matter what happened between them, she would always remember the magical Christmas she'd spent with Kit Lewis.

'I should probably go,' Kit said, downing the last dregs of his hot chocolate. 'I've had a lovely night, thank you. I feel well and truly Christmassy.'

He stood up and pulled on his coat.

'Wait,' Zoey blurted out before she'd put any thought into what she wanted to say.

He hesitated, his zip half pulled up.

She stood up. 'Kit, I don't think I want to be friends with you any more.'

He stared at her, his face falling. 'Shit, Zoey, did I do something wrong?'

'No, no, no.' She stepped up to him. 'You misunderstand. I really really bloody like you and I wonder if you'd like to… upgrade our relationship?'

His eyebrows shot up. 'I was kind of enjoying being your friend.'

'You don't want to upgrade?' She felt the disappointment flood through her.

'Oh god, I do but… I'm not great at being in a relationship and I don't want to lose you when it all goes wrong.'

'I don't think we need to assume it will go wrong, we can hope that it will go right.'

'Yes, true.' He sounded doubtful, which was not quite the reaction she was hoping for.

'Well, think about it. I totally understand if you'd like to stay friends, but if you ask me out, I promise the answer will be yes,' Zoey said, feeling a bit embarrassed now.

Kit turned to the door and then turned back.

'I don't need to think about it,' he said. 'I am worried about getting involved in a relationship again, especially with someone as magnificent as you, but love is a risk and I'd rather take that risk with you than with anyone else. Would you like to go out on a date with me?'

She grinned. 'Yes, absolutely.'

'Tomorrow night, after the market closes?'

'Yes, I'd love that.'

He nodded and moved to the door, opening it.

Zoey took a step back because outside was a complete blizzard, gusting through the door, the cold whipping in and immediately filling the room. Snow was falling so heavy outside she couldn't even see the lake.

'Wow, this wasn't forecast. The weather said we might have a few flakes, nothing like this,' she said. They'd obviously been so caught up in their lovely evening and feeding each other mince pies that they hadn't noticed the weather changing. Despite the fact the snow was coming down with a vengeance, there was something wonderfully exciting about it. She'd wanted a thick blanket of snow and it was looking like she'd get her wish. Although the weather was hardly practical.

'You can't go out in this,' Zoey said.

Kit stared at the snow falling thick and fast. 'It's only a ten-minute walk to the hotel. I'll probably be OK.'

The wind howled across the lake and Zoey shivered. 'Stay here tonight. That feels like a much safer option.'

He stared at the snow a moment longer. 'Are you sure?'

'Yes of course, it's just not worth going out in this.'

He closed the door and shrugged out of his coat. 'I think you're right. I'll sleep on the sofa.'

Zoey thought about this for a moment. She hadn't really thought through the invitation to stay. 'I don't have any spare blankets. It's a one-bedroom cottage. You can sleep in my bed with me.'

She watched his eyebrows shoot up into his hair.

'We can sleep in the same bed without mauling each other. We can be sensible about this. We're just going to sleep, nothing else. It's a fairly big bed too.'

'This upgrade just came with a very big bonus,' Kit said.

Zoey laughed. 'Come on. I do have a spare toothbrush to offer you if nothing else. I always bring a spare in case my electric one stops working. You can use the bathroom first.'

She turned the lights off and walked up the stairs; a few seconds later she heard Kit follow her.

'Here's the bedroom and there's the bathroom. The spare toothbrush is on the side.'

'Thanks,' Kit said, awkwardly, and went in and shut the door.

Zoey quickly got changed into her reindeer pyjamas and a few minutes later Kit came out of the bathroom wearing just his shorts and a t-shirt. She could tell he was nervous and she found that so damned endearing.

'Cute jammies,' Kit said.

She grinned. 'I'll just be a few minutes.'

She went into the bathroom, washed her face and cleaned her teeth and walked into the bedroom to find Kit already lying in bed.

She slipped into bed next to him and rolled on her side to face him.

'Is this OK?'

He rolled to face her too. 'Yes, it's fine. I mean the last woman I had in my bed was my ex-wife so it's a little weird. I certainly wasn't expecting this to happen tonight but at the same time it feels so right being here too.'

She smiled. 'It doesn't feel weird to me.' She shuffled a bit closer and he watched her. 'Did you cuddle your ex-wife in bed, or are you one of those men that doesn't like to be touched while you sleep?'

'My ex-wife wasn't big on cuddling. I quite like it,' Kit said, carefully.

She shuffled closer to see if he had any objections and, when he made none, she moved so her head was on his chest, her arm around his stomach. She lay there for a moment watching the snow swirl outside the window as she listened to his heart, which was racing against his chest. He wrapped an arm round her shoulders, holding her close, and she smiled.

'Goodnight,' Zoey said.

'Goodnight.'

Kit kissed her on the forehead, making her heart soar, before reaching over and switching off the bedside lamp, plunging them into darkness. The snow outside made the room lighter than it was normally and her eyes quickly became accustomed to the dark. She looked up at him and he was smiling at her.

'This upgrade just keeps getting better and better,' Kit said.

She smiled and put her head back on his chest, closing her eyes.

Things were moving very fast between Kit and her but nothing had ever felt so right before. She wanted to see what was going to happen between them. He was right, love was a risk, but she got the feeling that he was definitely worth it.

CHAPTER 7

20 DECEMBER

Zoey woke the next morning to an empty bed but, judging from the smells drifting up from the kitchen, Kit wasn't far away.

She got washed and dressed and wandered down to the kitchen to find him making French toast.

He smiled when he saw her and gave her a one-armed hug and a kiss on top of her head.

'You don't have to make me breakfast every day, you know, I could make you something one day. Although I have to say my efforts wouldn't look anywhere near as nice as that French toast does.'

'I want to thank you for letting me stay,' Kit said.

'Oh, there was no way I was turfing you out in that weather. Have you looked outside yet, are we snowed in?'

'It has stopped snowing and it looks quite deep, but I think we should make it through OK. I don't think Lindsey will be too impressed if I tell her I can't get to the hut because of the snow.'

'I don't know, sounds pretty plausible. We could stay

here and finish off the mince pies and watch Christmas movies all day.'

'Very tempting. I bet, with your love of Christmas, this kind of snow is right up your street.'

'I love snow, sledging, making snowmen, having snowball fights. We don't get enough of it, so you have to make the most of it when you can. When I was a child I tried freezing it in the hope it would last forever, but it never worked and soon the weather would change and that magic would melt away.'

'Well we definitely need to make the most of this stuff then.'

He turned his attention to the French toast as he dished it up onto plates. She noticed that on the table was a small vase with one of the flowers from the Christmas tree inside.

'What's this?'

'Well, I figured that now we have upgraded, our breakfast should be a romantic one. I thought flowers and ideally a candle for the middle of the table.'

'I have candles,' Zoey said, going to one of the kitchen drawers and grabbing one of the tiny pink birthday cake candles that had probably been left by one of the previous guests at the cottage. She lit it on the gas stove and then let wax drip onto a plate before welding the candle to the hot wax so it would stand up.

He grinned. 'Perfect.'

They sat down at the table and started eating. The French toast was delicious.

'And do you plan to woo me over the breakfast table?' Zoey said.

Kit cleared his throat. 'What would wooing involve? Do you want me to kiss you while we're eating breakfast? Because that could get messy.'

She suddenly wanted him to kiss her but it felt like it was too soon when they'd only just upgraded.

'Maybe we should build up to that, seeing as we already slept together. We should save something for the first date,' she said.

'Good idea. Gives me time to practise my technique.'

Zoey laughed in outrage. 'On who?'

'Oh no, I meant... I didn't mean I was going to kiss a load of other women.'

'Glad to hear it.'

He turned his attention back to his breakfast and she could see he was embarrassed. God, she really liked him.

'So where are we going on our first date tonight?' Zoey asked.

He chewed on his breakfast for a moment. 'Where would you like to go?'

She smiled. 'Why don't you surprise me.'

He groaned. 'What every man dreads to hear.'

She laughed. 'What? Why?'

'We don't want to surprise you women, what if we get it wrong? There's too much pressure. We'd rather be told what to do and then we do it. This is our first date, it has to go well or there won't be a second one. If I surprise you with a fish restaurant and you hate fish, it isn't going to go down well. If I take you to a restaurant and actually you'd prefer to go skydiving, then the restaurant is going to be pretty tame in comparison.'

'I'm fairly easy when it comes to food,' Zoey said. 'And definitely no skydiving.'

'OK,' Kit said, slowly. She could almost see his brain working as he thought. 'Or you could just tell me where you want to go and then the only thing I have to worry about is not boring you to death with my personality.'

'I don't think there's any fear of that,' Zoey said.

'I think there's every fear of that,' Kit said.

The way he said it made her think he'd been told he was boring in the past. She found that hard to believe.

She reached across the table and took his hand. 'Kit, I really like you. If I had been bored by you I wouldn't have wanted an upgrade. I also wouldn't be cuddling up to you over breakfast, I'd be thinking of some excuse to get you out of here. And I'm really looking forward to tonight because I get to spend more time with you, wherever we are. You don't have to worry about selling me the best version of yourself because I'm already sold.'

He stared at her then cleared his throat. He took a big swig of coffee and nearly choked on it.

He nodded and finally spoke. 'OK.'

'Good, now we better get a move on as I want to make a snowman before we go to the market and before all the snow melts. I think it would be good for your Christmas rehabilitation.'

He smiled. 'In that case we better do it.'

Zoey loved working with acrylics. She loved mixing various colours to get different shades and tones. She had enough experience of painting to know almost exactly how much yellow, orange, white and red she'd need to mix together to get the perfect shade of sand or what colours she'd need for a stormy sky, but she could have played with mixing paint colours together for hours and not get bored. It was soothing and helped to calm her mind. It was probably why Mike's TV show had been so popular: watching someone paint was soothing and relaxing.

Zoey loved the end result of working with acrylics too, it was so bold and bright and just not something you could replicate with watercolours.

She had already finished the painting of the lake that morning, recreating the colours of the lake as best she could, and now she was working on a village scene. Little houses with golden windows, the snow which she knew she'd add a sprinkling of glitter to when it was finished, the Christmas trees, sparkling with brightly coloured baubles. It was the layers of different-coloured paints that helped to make it look more real. Even something like the sea was not just made up of one colour blue; there were touches of cerulean, sky blue, ultramarine, cobalt, sapphire, Prussian blue, violet and even hints of emerald and viridian green too. Plus white of course – white was the colour she used more than any other to blend with the base colours to get the shades she wanted.

She stepped back to look at her work. This one was of Jewel Island and she absolutely loved it. The comedy she was so famous for in her paintings came courtesy of several people in different parts of the image. There were lots more details she wanted to add and she knew it would take a few more days, but she wanted to take her time to get it right.

Her phone suddenly burst into life. She wiped her hands and fished it out of her pocket to see it was her mum. She quickly answered it.

'Hey Mum, how you doing?'

'I'm all good, my lovely, how are you?'

'I'm good too. Made a few sales today which is always nice.'

'You have such a lovely talent, I'm sure you'll make many more,' her mum said. 'Have you seen Kit today?'

Zoey hesitated. She didn't want to tell her mum that they'd spent two nights sleeping together, her mum would be rushing out to buy a hat for the wedding.

'Briefly, this morning,' Zoey said, which was at least truthful, even if she had left out the fact she'd seen him in her house.

'I like him.'

'I do too. He's just so lovely,' Zoey said. 'We're actually going out on a date tonight.'

Her mum squealed excitedly and Zoey smiled as she held the phone away from her ear for a moment.

'Don't get too excited. It's just a date. It might end horribly.'

She didn't think it would but she was trying not to get too excited about it either. She didn't want to get her hopes up and then have them dashed.

'Where are you going?' her mum asked and Zoey could almost imagine her sitting down to get all the details.

'I don't know, I asked him to surprise me.'

'Zoey! That's mean. You know what men are like when it comes to surprises. Have you seen *Don't Tell the Bride?*'

Zoey laughed. 'All he has to do is pick somewhere for us to go. He can't go too far wrong, no matter what he chooses.'

'Where would you like to go? There's that new fancy Italian in the village.'

'That would be lovely if he chose somewhere like that. But you know what I'm like. I'd be happy with a bag of fish and chips while sitting on the beach and then maybe an ice cream at Cones at the Cove after. I don't need all the trimmings.'

'Come on, you want him to put in a bit of effort. Fish and chips doesn't really say romance, does it?'

'But I'm not bothered what the date actually entails, as long as it's not something crazy. I just want to have time to talk to him and get to know him. And I like fish and chips. What could be more romantic than a moonlit stroll on the beach? Maybe we'd have to cuddle together to keep warm.'

'OK, when you put it like that, it does sound pretty romantic. Although I doubt he will set the bar that low. I'm sure he'll want to pull out all the bells and whistles to impress you.'

'And that's OK too. I won't judge him on it. Whatever he chooses I'll be happy with.'

'Well, you'll have to tell me all about it. I want all the details,' her mum said.

'And I promise you'll have them. Well, perhaps a slightly edited version.'

'Fair enough, there are some things a mum doesn't need to know.'

Zoey laughed. 'I don't think it will get that far tonight.'

'Good, you should save some things for the second date.'

Zoey smiled. They said their goodbyes. Her stomach fluttered with butterflies as she thought about her date. For the first time in a long time she had something to look forward to.

'Earth to Kit.'

Kit blinked and realised his sister was talking to him. 'Sorry, what?'

Lindsey rolled her eyes with a smile. 'You've had that silly inane grin on your face all morning. What's going on?'

Kit hesitated in telling her he had a date; she'd make a big deal about it and he wasn't sure if it was yet. It felt like Zoey was holding back and understandably so after what happened with her fiancé. But then Lindsey would definitely find out anyway, she was like Sherlock Holmes for digging out every little detail of his life, whether he wanted to share it or not.

He took a deep breath. 'I have a date tonight.'

'Oh my god, I knew it. All this silly "just friends" malarkey. I knew you'd both come to your senses. The chemistry between you both just sizzles. Wait, it is with Zoey, right?'

'Yes, it's with Zoey.'

'I love that she agreed to go on a date with you after you threw a bucket of water all over her. I've never thought about throwing a bucket of water over a man to attract their attention before but she obviously liked it.'

'I don't think it was that that attracted her to me. Come to think of it, I'm not sure what attracted her to me.'

'You don't see your worth, do you, but you're a bloody amazing man. You obviously made a good impression on her.'

He sighed. 'You're my sister, you're probably a bit biased. My wife wanted a divorce after eight months of marriage, I certainly didn't make a good impression on her.'

'That's because she was screwing around with another man. That's on her, not you,' Lindsey said in exasperation. Probably because they'd had this conversation many times before.

'Yes, but what made her want to start screwing around in the first place? I clearly wasn't holding her attention.'

Kit thought back to when Lily had said she wanted a divorce and when he'd asked why she had told him that if she stayed with him she'd always regret it, that she knew she was missing out on bigger and better things. That's when she told him about Dante, he was apparently better at *everything*.

'*I deserve to have amazing sex, Kit, and I'm not going to settle for less than that any more,*' Lily had said, which had been hugely devastating to hear.

His girlfriends previous to Lily always seemed to have a good time with him in the bedroom. He was almost tempted to ring them up and ask them if the sex had really been bad but he wasn't a glutton for punishment. Although as Lily had reeled off a big, long list of things that Dante was better at, it seemed sex wasn't the only issue she'd had with Kit. It didn't fill him with a ton of confidence.

'Don't put Lily's issues on you,' Lindsey said. 'I'm friends with her sister and I know that since she left you Lily has been through more men than I've had hot dinners. She obviously gets bored easily. Give this date with Zoey a fair chance, don't go into it thinking it will end badly before it's even started.'

Kit nodded and smiled. His little sister did have some pearls of wisdom occasionally.

'She's the artist from number nine, isn't she?' Lindsey said.

'Yes, that's right.'

'You know, I walked past there this morning as she was setting up and her stuff really reminds me of Dad's.'

Kit frowned. 'Are you saying she's copied him?'

'No, of course not. It's different enough that it's definitely her style not Dad's, but it has that whimsical, kooky twist which Dad did so well. Plus it's all seaside villages, which were Dad's forte. It just made me think of him, that's all.'

'I haven't seen any of her art yet, I'll have to have a look. But there are enough artists out there that make their living from seaside paintings. That kind of thing is very popular.'

'That's true. I imagine quite a few of the newer artists might have been inspired by Dad's work. Every time I see a village painting I think of him but these were so similar in so many ways.' Lindsey paused. 'I wish we hadn't sold his paintings.'

'I do too,' Kit said.

After his dad had died, the art gallery where his paintings had been on display had eventually closed down. There were no other galleries interested in taking them so they had sat in the spare room at his parents' house for a year, which hadn't seemed right for such a celebrated artist. Then his mum had started talking about selling them so other people could enjoy his legacy. So they'd sold the lot; most of the money had gone to a stroke charity his dad had supported heavily while he was alive and his mum had gone on a cruise with her sister, something she'd always talked about doing with his dad. Now Mum was gone, the cruise remembered only with a few photos in an album, and his dad's paintings were scattered around the world. The only thing they had were the prints they sold on his website to those that remembered him. There was very little of his legacy left.

'Maybe it's a good thing if Zoey was inspired by Dad's work,' Kit said. 'His art lives on in her.'

Lindsey nodded. 'I like that.'

CHAPTER 8

Zoey was just locking up when Kit came hurrying over with a bunch of white roses, mixed with holly leaves and red berries. It looked stunning.

'Happy first date,' Kit said, offering them out to her.

She smiled. 'Thank you, these are lovely.'

'I figured flowers were probably a bit safer than a maternity jumper.'

Zoey laughed. 'I have something for you too.'

She handed him the paper bag. He took it and pulled out the small canvas she'd finished working on that morning: the picture of the lake, the frozen shades of blue and the glittering snow from the night before.

'This is beautiful,' Kit said, softly. 'You've captured the beauty of the lake perfectly. I will treasure this always as a reminder of the night we upgraded.'

Zoey laughed.

He offered out his arm and she took it. He was so sweet.

Marika gave her the thumbs up as she locked up her

own stand. Zoey laughed as Marika gave her an elaborate wink too.

'Now, I'm not sure what you have in mind, but if it's somewhere fancy, do I have time to nip home and get changed?' Zoey asked.

Kit looked at her for a moment. 'Zoey, you look lovely and, as it happens, you are perfectly dressed for what I have planned.'

'Ooh, I'm intrigued,' Zoey said.

The little village was adorned with Christmas lights and decorations swinging from the trees and wreaths hanging from the vintage style lampposts. It looked beautiful. The streets were pretty quiet as well, everyone tucked up inside out of the cold, which made their first date even more magical. Although she suspected the pubs and restaurants would be quite full of people enjoying the festivities.

They walked towards the new Italian her mum had talked about and heavenly smells drifted out the door. The place looked more classy than welcoming, but the food smelt amazing and those tucking into their meals sitting in the window seemed to be enjoying it. She could certainly put up with somewhere posh for food like that.

But to her surprise they kept going straight past it.

She looked back over her shoulder as they walked past at a wonderful-looking seafood pasta dish that had just been served to one of the customers. Maybe she had judged that place too harshly.

'I thought we'd keep it simple tonight,' Kit said, watching her gaze.

'Simple is great,' Zoey said, and then smiled when they walked up to the fish and chip shop.

'These fish and chips are the best I've ever tasted,' Kit said. 'The fish is fresh and they cook everything to order, instead of it sitting under the hot lamps for hours. I thought we could eat them down on the beach.'

'That sounds lovely,' Zoey said, quietly marvelling over how Kit could get it so perfectly right.

'Cod and chips OK?'

'Yes, thank you,' Zoey said, rooting in her bag for her purse.

'It's OK, I've got this,' he said, walking into the shop.

She watched him with a smile. Kit was someone she could very easily fall for but she couldn't believe it was this easy. What were the chances of bumping into someone where she happened to be working for just a few days and that person turning out to be her forever? Very unlikely. She had fallen in love with David so hard and so fast and look at how that had turned out. Maybe she could try to keep her heart in check and just enjoy this for what it was without seeing forever. It didn't have to be an all-or-nothing.

He came out with two parcels of fish and chips and passed her one. The paper was hot to the touch and she juggled it between her hands until she got used to the temperature.

'Let's go down here,' Kit said, gesturing to the nearest set of steps that would take them onto the beach.

She followed him down the steps onto the sand. It was dark down here but the moon was casting sparkling ribbons across the waves. It looked enchanting.

Kit guided her towards the back of the beach and she

stopped when she saw candles had been lit in storm lanterns inside a cave.

'Kit!' Zoey gasped. 'Did you do this?'

'Yes, I thought we should probably have some light and the cave gives us some shelter from the elements.'

She walked closer. There was a blanket on the floor just inside the mouth of the cave and several more storm lanterns inside, casting a warm flickering golden light across the cave walls.

She swallowed a lump in her throat. It was strange how something so small could mean so much. When she'd been with David there had never been anything like this. No romantic gestures, or any dates that he had put any real effort into other than taking her to a restaurant. This was infinitely better.

'Thank you, this is so wonderful,' Zoey said.

Kit gestured for her to sit down and, as she did, he wrapped another blanket around her shoulders before sitting down next to her. He was so thoughtful.

She tore open one end of her parcel and started eating the chips. Kit did the same. The chips *were* really good, just as he said.

'I thought, after, we could walk down to Cones at the Cove and have one of their ice creams,' Kit said, popping a chip in his mouth.

She paused, a piece of fish halfway to her mouth as the penny dropped. 'Oh my god, you spoke to my mum, didn't you?'

Kit promptly choked on his chip. 'Shit. I thought the ice creams might give it away. Your mum came to see me straight after she got off the phone to you. And I wasn't going to look a gift horse in the mouth.'

Zoey laughed. 'The little minx.'

'I gave her free churros for the information, so I wasn't innocent in all of this. The candles were all me though. I thought it made it more romantic.'

'The candles make it perfect. So would you have thought of this on your own?'

'Maybe in the summer, when it's a bit warmer. I wouldn't have thought of doing this in the winter. But the cave certainly protects us from most of the elements.'

'The cave was an excellent idea. So where would you have taken me tonight before my mum interfered?'

'I was all set to take you to that Italian place, but she said it was too posh for you.'

Zoey nodded. 'And I'd have been more than happy with that. I did think it was a bit posh but, considering the food we just saw when we were walking past, I think I might have judged the place too soon.'

'We'll have to go there on our second date,' Kit said.

She smiled. She already knew there would be a second date with him and a third. 'I look forward to it.'

They ate in silence for a while and Zoey couldn't help but smile at how he'd carried out her hopes for the date to the letter. Even if he had cheated considerably, it was lovely that he wanted to make her happy. And the cave and the candles were the cherry on the top. She really bloody liked Kit Lewis. He was a wonderful man.

'So why are you single?' Zoey asked. 'You said your brother bought you that t-shirt with the snowmen having sex because you'd been single for a long time. Aside from

134

throwing buckets of water over potential dates, you seem like a lovely, sweet guy.'

'I guess women don't want to settle for lovely and sweet, they want dynamic, passionate, exciting. I don't think I tick that box for them.'

She thought about that for a moment. Did women really want that? Of course passion had its place, to have that connection, that chemistry, desire for each other was an important part of a relationship. But she'd had that excitement with David – they hadn't been able to keep their hands off each other in the first few months but there'd been very little chance for talking or getting to know each other. She barely knew him when she'd accepted his proposal, so swept up in the moment. The reality of that relationship was far different. David had always been looking for the next new and exciting thing. The next sporting craze, the newest piece of technology, the latest gadget, *the* new phone that everyone had to have. He had a whole room filled with discarded gadgets and equipment that had served their purpose for a few months before he'd found a new fad to whet his appetite. As it turned out, he treated women exactly the same. He'd get caught up in the excitement of a new woman and then discard them as soon as he'd had his fill. Lots of ex-girlfriends came out of the woodwork after she and David broke up, to tell her she wasn't the first girlfriend he'd cheated on and certainly wouldn't be the last. And although he was ploughing headfirst into this wedding, the latest fad he wanted to try, there were already rumours that he was screwing around with someone else.

Zoey didn't want or need that kind of excitement in her life.

'I don't know what will happen between us, Kit, whether what we have now will turn out to be forever, but if we do end up married further down the line, I can categorically promise you that I would not be *settling* with you. I would consider myself very lucky to spend the rest of my life with someone like you.'

He stared at her for a moment. 'My wife didn't share that sentiment. She asked me for a divorce less than a year after we got married. I think she found me boring. Although there've been several men since me, she apparently found all of them boring as well.'

'Sounds like my ex-fiancé. Low attention span, but that's his issue not mine. Same with you, it's not your fault if married life was not for her. Don't let that bring you down.'

'None of my relationships have lasted long. I can't help wondering if the problem is me.'

'Well, you can stop thinking that right now,' Zoey said. 'It's really hard to find someone you can connect with on that level. Someone you can really imagine forever with. There are millions of people on this planet – just because two people are single and find each other attractive doesn't mean that they have anything in common or share a connection strong enough for something long term.'

He sighed as he finished off his chips. 'I have no idea what I'm doing when it comes to relationships, I always feel like I'm second-guessing everything.'

'You turned up to our date tonight with flowers, you've set up this lovely picnic on the beach with candles. Trust me when I say you are doing everything right so far. You don't need to doubt yourself. You want me to give you a run-down of how you've done so far, for good or bad? OK, let's start from the beginning. Throwing a bucket of water over a potential date, not good, saving me from third-degree burns, actually pretty brilliant. Buying me a Christmas jumper to replace the one I'd ruined, very sweet, buying me a maternity jumper, laughably bad—'

'See, there are a lot of ups and downs there.'

'Not being put off by spending the evening with my mum,' Zoey went on as if she hadn't been interrupted. 'Genuinely talking and listening to her, to both of us, making me laugh a lot. Stripping down to your pants, well, I certainly appreciated that very much, throwing yourself on an icy lake to rescue a rabbit, well we can certainly tick the hero box. Spending the night in my house without trying to make it more than it was, so you have the respectful box ticked too. Making me breakfast twice, giving me those lovely morning hugs. This lovely date. Honestly, you're ticking every single box for me.'

She watched as a slow smile spread across his face. 'It feels like meeting you, for the first time in a long time, things are finally going right.'

'Maybe our stars have aligned,' Zoey said.

'Maybe.'

They sat staring at each other for the longest moment.

'Now would be a good time for our first kiss,' Zoey whispered theatrically.

He laughed. 'Oh no, I'm saving that for the end of the night.'

'The big finale?' Zoey said.

He rubbed the back of his neck, awkwardly. 'Something like that.'

She finished off her fish and chips and lay back on the blanket to look at the stars. After a moment Kit lay back with her and she snuggled against his chest. He wrapped an arm round her shoulder and kissed her forehead.

Zoey let out a sigh of contentment. 'This is the best first date I've had in a very long time.'

'We haven't even got to the grand finale yet,' Kit said, pulling the blanket up over her.

She smiled. 'I have no doubt that will be amazing.'

They walked hand in hand towards Cones at the Cove, a gorgeous little ice cream and dessert café in the grounds of the Sapphire Bay Hotel. It had a lovely beachy vibe to the place but Zoey's favourite thing was the wall of different-flavoured ice creams where people could build their own desserts and add a wonderful range of toppings too.

Kit pushed open the door and they were greeted by a woman in a blue Cones at the Cove t-shirt carrying a baby in a papoose who was fast asleep.

'Hello, I'm Skye, the manager here at Cones at the Cove,' the woman said, cheerily. 'This is my new apprentice, Thomas.' Skye stroked the baby's head affectionately. 'Who quite honestly sleeps all day and doesn't really pull his weight at all.'

Zoey laughed. 'You can't sack him though, he's too cute.'

'He does play that card very well,' Skye said. 'Now have you been to us before?'

'I have, with my mum a few weeks ago,' Zoey said.

'I haven't,' Kit said.

'OK, would you like me to give you the guided tour or...'

'I can show him around,' Zoey said.

'OK, great, here are two menus. You can choose desserts from there or build your own ice cream sundae from the wall over there,' Skye said, showing them to a table. 'I can recommend the mince pie waffles – my husband, Jesse, makes them and they are absolutely divine. Someone will be over shortly to take your order and get you some drinks.'

She left them to it as they settled themselves into a booth.

'All of their desserts are made fresh here, nothing is bought in,' Zoey said, opening her menu and then glancing over to the specials board. 'So you can't really go wrong.'

'What are you going for?' Kit asked, looking down the menu.

'The build your own dessert. There's a wall of fifty different-flavoured ice creams over there so you can come in here every week and have different combinations every time. You should see the choice of toppings too. It's every child's dream. And as I'm definitely still a big kid at heart, this place is ideal for me.'

'Sounds fun, let's do it.'

A waitress came over to take their order. They told her they were going to build their own and then she asked about drinks.

'What flavoured hot chocolates do you do?' Zoey asked. Snuggling up with Kit on the beach under the blankets had been kind of cosy for a while but now she needed something to warm her up and the ice cream wasn't going to do that.

'We have marshmallow and white chocolate, Christmas pudding, mince pie, After Eight, Toblerone, and we even have a sprout-flavoured one if you're feeling brave.'

'*Sprouts?*' Kit said, giving a shudder.

'Eww yes, I'd have to agree. I hate sprouts at the best of times, but I certainly don't want that in my hot chocolate.'

'It's definitely an acquired taste but some people like it,' the waitress said.

'I'll think I'll stick to the After Eight one please,' Zoey said.

'I'll take the Toblerone,' Kit said.

The girl nodded. 'I'll be back in a second with your bowls for the ice creams.'

'I love Toblerone,' Kit said. 'We'd all have one every Christmas, the bigger the better, and then, because it has such a distinctive triangular-shaped box, we'd all try to disguise it when we wrapped it in the most ingenious ways. One year, Adam wrapped one for our dad with his hand weights, so it weighed a ton and stuck out in lots of different angles. My mum wrapped one for me once inside a duvet. It was huge. Every year, we'd get more and more ridiculous with our attempts to disguise it. Dad was away a lot with his work but Christmas was the one time we all got together and celebrated. We haven't done the Toblerone thing since Mum and Dad died and I miss that.'

The waitress returned with their bowls and spoons and then left them alone again.

'Let's go and see what they've got,' Kit said, moving to get out of his seat.

'Hang on. I have a challenge for you,' Zoey said. 'You have to choose three flavoured ice creams that says something about you.'

'Oooh, I like that,' Kit said, his eyes sparking with amusement.

'And if you choose vanilla because you think you're boring and plain, I'm going to make you drink the sprout hot chocolate.'

He laughed. 'I promise, no vanilla.'

'I want more Toblerone stories from you, the things that mean something to you.'

He nodded. 'OK.'

They got up and moved over to the wall of ice cream. There were so many to choose from and she had to pick flavours that meant something to her, that told a story. Now she'd set the challenge, it was a lot harder than she'd first thought. It seemed Kit was having a difficult time choosing too.

Zoey selected one flavour and put a dollop of it into her bowl and glanced across at Kit, who was already adding his third flavour and heading over to the toppings bar.

This was tough.

She chose one more and was then just toying with getting the strawberry cheesecake flavour because that reminded her of a trip to San Francisco when she spotted something else which she knew instantly she had to have. Happy that her collection was complete, she went over to the toppings to add some chocolate buttons, fudge pieces and some M&Ms. She returned to their table to join Kit, who was nibbling on a bit of Flake.

'OK, what have you got?' Zoey said, sitting down opposite him.

'First up, I have Ferrero Rocher. That was always a Christmas treat in our house. There were three big boxes that would sit on the coffee table in the middle of the lounge, in their shiny gold paper, and I thought they were so fancy. There were those adverts with the glamorous parties and the ambassador who was spoiling his guests with Ferrero Rocher. I thought we must be really rich if we could afford those. We'd have one each night on each day of December and it just felt really special. Dad was away at weekends with his gallery so we'd save them for him on the days he wasn't there. When he came back, he always used to give his saved ones to us or Mum. Even now, when I see them in a shop and I can buy them for a couple of quid, it still makes me feel special to have them.'

Zoey smiled. 'I love that. And Ferrero Rocher ice cream sounds lovely.'

'Please, help yourself,' Kit said.

She leaned across the table and took a small spoonful. It tasted delicious.

'OK, what's the second flavour?' she said.

'Watermelon. Again, another childhood memory of sitting in the garden in the summer, with my brother and sister, having a slice each, picking out the black seeds and later planting them in the garden in the hope we could grow watermelon trees. Laughing when the red juice would go everywhere. It's such a distinctive flavour that I always remember those summers, eating watermelon with my siblings. Life was much simpler back then.'

'Agreed. Those summer holidays used to last forever, and the only issue you had to deal with was whether your bike got a puncture.'

'Oh yes, I knew my puncture repair kit like the back of my hand,' Kit laughed. 'The final flavour is macadamia nut. Because I first tried them on a trip to Australia and it was probably the best holiday I've ever been on.'

'Oh, I've been there too, where did you go, what did you do, why did you love it so much?'

Kit laughed. 'Why don't you tell me about your ice cream flavours before they all melt and then we can talk about Australia.'

'Good point. So firstly I have candyfloss-flavoured ice cream. It just reminds me of trips to the fair when I was younger: the rides, the smells, trying to win an oversized teddy bear. We'd always get a bag of candyfloss and I used to love how it'd melt on my tongue.'

'Ah yes, fairground memories. I always used to go on the waltzers and then have to lie down for ages after because my head didn't stop spinning. I used to love the haunted house or the ghost train, because you never knew what to expect.'

Zoey laughed. 'Mostly model skeletons that would launch themselves from cupboards. It was the things that touched your head in the darkness that used to freak me out.'

'Yes, it was always the things you couldn't see that were the scariest. What's your second flavour?'

'Apple pie. My mum's apple pie is the best, we'd have it

with ice cream or custard and it just always reminded me of home. That smell, when I'd walk through the doors after school, was just heaven. We'd have it most weekends, mainly because Mum's friend used to like it and he was always there at weekends.'

'My dad loved apple pie too,' Kit said. 'We'd always have it when he came home. And Mum made her pastry from scratch.'

Zoey laughed.

'OK, final flavour?'

'Churro flavour,' Zoey smiled.

He paused, his spoon halfway to his mouth. He cleared his throat. 'Why did you choose that?'

'Oh, I think churros could be my new favourite thing.'

He stared at her and then slowly ate the mouthful of ice cream on his spoon, his eyes locked with hers.

'Regardless of what happens between us, churros will always remind me of the lovely man I met at the Christmas market when he threw a bucket of water over me.'

Kit laughed and the tension was gone. 'You're never going to let me forget that, are you?'

'For as long as we both shall live.'

Zoey couldn't help smiling as they walked back to Moonstone Cottage. As first dates went, tonight's had been pretty perfect. The fish and chips on the beach, the candles, the ice cream, but mostly the talking non-stop as they got to know each other had been wonderful. She couldn't believe how everything just clicked for them, how easy it was to spend time together. Whereas before she had been cautious of jumping into another relationship again, especially one that seemed to have a cut-off point, once the Christmas market came to an end, she was now eager to see where this one was going to lead. She didn't want to hold back, keeping her heart locked away for fear of getting hurt, she wanted to enjoy her time with Kit with no reservations.

They reached the cottage door and she looked up at the night sky as snow fell gently around them, topping up the blanket of white that had covered the lake and the rest of the island the night before. It was beautiful, glittering in the darkness.

She glanced at Kit and could see he was worried and she knew why.

'Kit Lewis, why do you look so terrified?'

'You know why,' Kit said. 'There's a hell of a lot riding on this first kiss.'

She smiled and shook her head. 'No, there isn't. I promise you there will be a second date and a third because I'm really enjoying spending time with you.'

'What if there is no spark?'

'Oh, I'm pretty damn sure there will be a spark,' Zoey said. The more time she'd spent with him that night, the more she was attracted to him. Just the thought of kissing him now was making her heart race.

'What if I kiss like a wet fish?'

Zoey laughed. 'I'm sure that won't be the case but, if it is, then we'll talk about it.'

He ran his hand through his hair and she decided to put

him out of his misery. She took hold of the collar of his coat, leaned up and kissed him.

He paused for the briefest of seconds before he was kissing her back.

God, this kiss was wonderful. She'd expected it to be lovely and sweet because the man himself was, but this was... perfect. She reached up to stroke his face as he moved his hands to her waist and then she slid her hand round the back of his neck, caressing the hair there in the gentlest of touches.

She wasn't sure at what point the kiss changed and whether she had instigated that change or he had, but suddenly the kiss turned urgent, passionate, a sudden desperate desire for him ripping through her. He let out a little moan of need and held her closer as he pinned her against the door. Christ, this was the hottest kiss she'd ever had and she'd had some good kisses in her life.

He pulled back slightly to look at her, his breath heavy against her lips. She was wrapped around him so tight that he could barely move at all and she forced herself to let him go.

Her breathing was unsteady, she was so completely turned on that it took her a few moments to form words in her mouth.

'Bloody hell,' she whispered and then let out a laugh of shock.

He brushed his hand through his hair and stepped back a little. 'You laughing after our first kiss is not a good sign.'

She shook her head, touching her lips where he had burned her with his kiss. 'It's a very good sign, but Christ Kit, you can't kiss someone like that on a first date.'

'Kiss you like what?'

'Like you wanted to pin me to the nearest hard surface and do rude and wonderful things to me.'

Kit laughed nervously. 'I have to admit there was an element of that, I didn't mean there to be, but suddenly when I was kissing you, I couldn't stop thinking about… that.'

'I could tell, holy shit. Best first kiss I've ever had.'

His face lit up. 'Really?'

Zoey nodded. 'I never sleep with anyone on the first date, but all I could think about when I was kissing you was opening the cottage door and finishing that kiss properly.'

His eyes darkened with need, then he shook his head and turned away for a second as if trying to cool his thoughts. He turned back. 'OK, let me try this again. I promise I'll be more respectful this time, no sexy thoughts.'

He moved closer, his eyes asking for permission and she nodded. He cupped her face gently and kissed her. This was much softer, more tender, but those images of making love to him were already imprinted in her mind, the simple taste of him igniting a fire inside her and he was barely touching her. If he kissed like this, what would the main event be like?

No, she needed to stop those thoughts.

She pulled back slightly. 'I have had the most amazing night Kit Lewis, but I think you better go before I drag you inside and do rude and wonderful things to you.'

He nodded, kissed her on the forehead in the sweetest of kisses and then took a definite step back.

'Thank you for an incredible night,' Kit said, softly. 'I'll see you tomorrow.'

'You can count on that.'

He took another step back and she loved that he had the biggest smile on his face. He gave her a wave and turned away. She watched him go and he kept turning back to give her another wave. Eventually she went inside and then, because she couldn't help it, she watched him go through the window too. Right before he disappeared behind some trees, she swore she saw him do one of those little sideways kicks of joy and it filled her heart. She let out a little giggle.

She really bloody liked this man.

CHAPTER 9

21ST DECEMBER

When Zoey got to her stall the following morning, Marika was waiting for her with a cup of Christmas tea, one of Zoey's favourites from the market. She opened up her hut and then Marika passed her the mug, eyebrows raised expectantly.

Zoey took a long, deliberate sip. 'Thank you for the drink.'

'Oh come on,' Marika said. 'Nothing is free in this life. Give.'

Zoey laughed. 'Last night was wonderful, the perfect first date.' She looked over her shoulder as Sylvia, the elderly lady she'd met a few days before, walked in wearing a spectacular red velvet cloak. Sylvia walked to the back of the shop and started flicking through the paintings there. Zoey lowered her voice. 'At the end we shared a first kiss which was so incredible it was probably the best kiss of my life. I don't want to get carried away as it's only been a few days but this feels like something special.'

'Just enjoy yourself,' Marika said. 'We always worry

about the future and forget to enjoy the now. If it doesn't lead anywhere, if it fizzles out, at least you had fun in the next few weeks. There's not enough of that in our lives.'

Zoey smiled and she loved the sentiment. 'Thank you, I think you're right.' She glanced at Sylvia again, who was staring at Mike's paintings. 'I better go, but when I come back we can talk more about you and Elias.'

Marika batted her away affectionately.

Zoey went to the back of the shop and Sylvia smiled at her as she approached.

'Hello, we met a few days ago,' Sylvia said.

'I remember, Sylvia right?'

'Yes, Sylvia O'Hare.'

'Zoey Flynn,' Zoey shook her hand.

'These paintings are wonderful,' Sylvia gestured around the shop.

'Thank you.'

'And these two are Jack Ashley's if I'm not mistaken.'

Mike's signature on his paintings was far from clear. It started with a J, curled into an A and then there was an elaborate squiggle at the end. So unless you knew the work, you wouldn't know who the artist was. But for many his art was so distinctive it was very easily identifiable without the signature.

'They are,' Zoey said. 'Are you a fan of his work?'

'Oh yes, I love his art. I have two of the originals at my house.' Sylvia dug her phone out of her pocket and swiped the screen a few times and then showed Zoey the wonderful paintings she had in her house. It made Zoey smile that even after all these years, Mike's art was still appreciated. 'I met him a few times too, wonderful man.

These two that you have are slightly different to his others because of the flowers at the bottom. None of his others had that and I wondered why he decided to have flowers in these.'

Zoey cleared her throat. 'Maybe he just fancied doing something different. I know my paintings have evolved quite a lot over the years.'

'I imagine that's probably the reason,' Sylvia said. 'Although in the art world there were rumours of a collaboration, although Jack never admitted it. But look at the signatures, even those are slightly different. On the paintings at my house you have the normal squiggle at the end of his name that has those two big loops and a smaller one with that flourish underneath his name. But on yours, the flourish underneath looks more like a Z.'

Zoey tilted her head and pretended to look at the signature. 'Hmm, maybe he just got carried away with the flourish – you know, made it more elaborate. I know my own signature changes almost every time I do it.'

Sylvia watched her carefully. 'Are these originals?'

'Yes they are,' Zoey said.

'I've seen copies of these, but I haven't seen them in real life. I went to his gallery shortly after he died and looked at all of his collection, but these two weren't part of that.'

'No, I... acquired them before he died,' Zoey said, carefully.

'Now that's interesting,' Sylvia said, staring at her with astute eyes. 'Because Jack never sold his originals while he was alive. He was quite happy to make prints and copies but the originals hung in his gallery for everyone to enjoy them.'

'My mum was friends with him, neighbours actually, so he gave these to us as a gift.'

'Ah I see,' Sylvia said as if she saw a lot more than what Zoey had said.

She turned her attention back to Mike's paintings. 'It was such a shame about his stroke, his work was never the same after that. They were still good but a different kind of good.'

Zoey hesitated before she spoke because she could never give away Mike's secret, she would take that with her to the grave.

She cleared her throat. 'He did struggle after his stroke, painting didn't come easy to him any more and he so badly wanted to give people what they loved, what he was famous for.'

'Oh, when you said you were neighbours, I didn't realise you knew him so well.'

'We, erm... used to paint together.'

God, it felt like she was giving away too much. Sylvia had the kind of eyes that saw everything.

'You must have only been a child when he'd had his stroke.'

'Fourteen.' Zoey remembered it like it was yesterday, Mike sagging in his chair as he was painting with her, Zoey panicking that he was dead, calling the ambulance because her mum hadn't even been there at that time. Getting him on the floor and in a recovery position all by herself. It had been terrifying. And months after, when he'd been struggling to paint, she'd always wondered if she could have done more at the time to help him. Or if she'd somehow been to blame. He hadn't been himself when she'd suggested painting together, he'd been tired and wanted to have a lie-down. But she'd pleaded with him and he'd relented. She'd always wondered if she'd made him worse by not letting him rest.

'No one saw him paint after that,' Sylvia said. 'He used to paint in his gallery sometimes and people would come in and watch him, but he didn't after his stroke. And he stopped doing his TV show too. I didn't realise he was struggling.'

Mike *had* struggled. His right hand hadn't worked the same as it did before. And for many months he hadn't even wanted to try because, every time he had, his paintings had turned out very badly, at least in his eyes. He got so down about it. Zoey used to paint whenever he'd come round to encourage him not to give up. And then one day they came up with a solution to help him paint again. It had been Zoey's idea and it was like a huge load had been lifted from his shoulders. And although the paintings in the gallery were never the same as they had been before, he was happy again and that was the most important thing.

Sylvia turned back to look at Zoey's paintings. 'So you were inspired by him?'

'Yes. His work has a real charm, it made people smile, and I knew I wanted to do something like that.'

Sylvia nodded. 'You have a lovely style. I'm sure he would be very proud of you.'

'Oh no, it wasn't like that,' Zoey said, realising she was defending where there was no accusation.

Sylvia studied her. 'I just meant that, I'm sure he would be proud to know he has inspired a new generation of artists.'

Zoey nodded. 'I'm sure he would.'

Sylvia picked up one of Zoey's originals, showing a harbour scene with little boats taking a battering in the winter storms. Even the Christmas tree lights were hanging off in a haphazard way.

'I really like this one. It reminds me of Jewel Island.' Sylvia nodded thoughtfully. 'I'll take it.'

Zoey was impressed she hadn't even looked at the price label on the back.

Zoey moved over to the counter. 'Shall I wrap it for you?'

'Yes, please do, I want to make sure it gets home safely. Then I can hang it with my two Jack Ashley ones. It seems fitting that they should be together.'

Zoey didn't say anything as she wrapped the artwork in bubble wrap and then brown paper. She rang up the purchase on the till and handed Sylvia her new painting.

'Thank you.'

Sylvia nodded and made her way out the shop. She stopped at the entrance. 'By the way, I couldn't help over-hearing your conversation with your friend. Honey, if a man kisses that good on a first date, you want to hang onto him.'

Zoey smiled as Sylvia walked away but then the smile fell from her face as she tried to retrace the conversation. Had she said something too revealing? Sylvia definitely had a way about her that saw things you didn't really want to share.

She turned back to the paintings. Maybe she shouldn't have brought them to the market. She'd kept them in her home, hanging in her studio to inspire her when she did her own paintings. It seemed fitting to have them here with her too, almost as if having those paintings here would allow Mike to see her success. But she didn't want people to ask questions like Sylvia had or, worse, draw conclusions.

She carefully took them down from the wall and put them under the counter. It was safer that way.

'So how was the big date?' Lindsey said, as she finished serving a customer.

Kit grinned. 'Amazing. I honestly don't think it could have been more perfect.'

'Oh, so you and her... did you...?' she waggled her eyebrows mischievously.

He smiled. 'Did we...?'

'You know... did you plant the parsnip?'

He burst out laughing. 'What the hell?'

'Did you practise your parallel parking? Did you do the hot yoga dance? Did you enter her castle? Did you fill her gas tank?'

He laughed. 'You are such a bloke, and no, there was no entering castles or planting parsnips or any other euphemisms.'

'You said it was the perfect date,' Lindsey said.

'It can be perfect without sex. We just connect in a way I've never known before, not even with Lily. She makes me happier than I've felt in a long time, maybe forever.'

Lindsey stared at him. 'You're falling for her? After one date? You don't know her.'

155

'There's nothing hidden when it comes to Zoey, no secrets. She's a very open and honest person.'

'Everyone has secrets,' Lindsey said.

'I don't think Zoey does.'

'Look, I'm happy for you. You need someone lovely after Lily broke your heart. Have fun with her, do the bedroom rodeo, but you don't need to leap ahead to marriage and babies. Try to keep your heart in check for now. I don't want to see you getting hurt.'

Kit nodded but he wasn't sure how he could put the brakes on. He had feelings for Zoey that went way beyond anything he'd ever experienced before.

'I spoke to Craig by the way,' Lindsey said, as she stocked up some of the containers for the crêpe toppings.

'Oh?'

'He's coming for lunch the day after tomorrow. He's staying at the Sapphire Bay Hotel, so I said we'd meet him there at one in the restaurant.'

Kit let out a heavy breath. 'OK.'

'You don't sound too happy.'

'I just don't think this will be a good thing.'

'Just try to keep an open mind.'

He nodded. He'd try.

The snow that had covered the island over the last few days had largely melted by the end of the day, which was a real shame. Zoey had hoped that it might stick around for Christmas Day, but the winter sun had come out in force and turned most of it to a grey slush. It was also a shame for the Great Big Snowball Fight, which the hotel was organising in the hotel gardens, because if the snow had stuck around for a few more hours they could have used the real stuff rather than the fake stuff that had been piled up liberally outside the hotel.

Zoey and Kit were lining up along with other guests and market stall holders. She could see Marika laughing with Elias a little bit further down the garden and it made her smile to see her friend so happy. She wondered if, once Christmas was out the way, whether Marika and Elias would have any kind of future together, or if it was more like Marika said, something to enjoy for now rather than worry about the future.

She looked at Kit. She really wanted to just enjoy this for what it was now but she couldn't help having hope for the future too. She really wanted this to work. She didn't want to walk away from him after Christmas. Was it silly to want forever with him when she barely knew him? She shook her head. She needed to take a leaf out of Marika's book and just enjoy the now, not worry about the future.

'What is this stuff anyway?' Kit said, oblivious to what was in her head. He knelt down to touch the fake snow.

'I wondered that myself,' said a man standing next to Kit. 'This is a company that provides snow specifically for snowball fights around the country. The normal insta-snow you get from toy shops is made from a harmless sodium polyacrylate, I looked it up. But that stuff isn't great for making snowballs, it doesn't clump together like normal snow does. This stuff has a special ingredient which helps it stick together more.'

Zoey and Kit stared at the man. He seemed to know a lot about fake snow.

'Sorry, I'm Noah, I own the hotel with my wife Aria and her sisters.'

'I'm Zoey. We're each running one of the stands in the market.'

'I'm Kit.'

Noah shook their hands. 'Good to meet you. I looked into this snow a lot when we were organising the Christmas market. Sadly my brain stores all that useless information. I'm assured that this stuff is safe, but there is a possibility that the effect of the real snow on it might make it gloopy and sticky. It certainly doesn't look as fresh as when it was delivered a few days ago. We did think about cancelling but I know a lot of people are looking forward to it.'

'Ah, it'd be a shame not to do it. Although if the weather had pulled its finger out, we could have had real snow for our snowball fight,' Zoey said.

'I know, I was so pleased when it snowed the other night. I can't believe the sun has come out after that blizzard we had,' Noah said. 'Oh, here's Aria.'

A woman came over with a little girl.

'Aria, this is Zoey and Kit from the market,' Noah said. 'This is Aria and our daughter Orla.'

'Hello,' Aria said. 'Oh hang on, you're our viral superstars, aren't you?'

Kit laughed. 'We're hoping to remain incognito.'

'What does in-cog-nee-toe mean?' Orla said, sounding out each syllable separately.

'It means I don't want anyone to know who I am,' Kit

said.

Orla wrinkled her little nose. 'Why do you not want anyone to know who you are?'

'Because I have a secret identity,' Kit whispered theatrically.

'He's a superhero,' Zoey said.

Orla looked at them both with wide eyes and then gave a snort of disbelief. 'I don't think so.'

She turned her attention to another man who had come to join them, who swept her up in his arms. 'Angel!' Orla shrieked with delight. 'Are you coming to play snowballs with us?'

'I am.'

'Are Clover and Pearl coming to play too?' Orla asked.

'Pearl is only four weeks old, so she's probably a little young to play with snowballs, so my sister is going to look after her for a bit, but Clover is coming and Skye and Jesse will be here in a moment, and Bea.'

'Yayy! I love Bea,' Orla said.

'Angel,' Aria said. 'This is Kit and Zoey, our viral superstars.'

Angel looked over at them with a grin. 'Hello, sorry about the viral thing. We're still getting comments now about it. Quite a few women want to know who you are, especially Kit. We've had comments like "Give him my number, he can save me anytime." Are you single?'

Kit laughed and Zoey felt a pang of jealousy.

'I'm not, I'm afraid. My girlfriend wouldn't be too impressed if I was giving out my number to lots of women.'

Zoey felt her eyes widen. Girlfriend? That felt like their upgrade had suddenly got a lot more serious. They'd been on one date, did he really think of her as his girlfriend? But actually, the more she considered it, the more she found herself liking that label, even if Kit hadn't thought about it to that extent. He was just trying to put Angel off.

Aria looked at them, her eyes narrowed. 'And there's no romance between you two?'

'We're friends,' Zoey said, firmly, and was grateful to see Skye approaching with two people – a young teenage girl and someone who was presumably her husband Jesse. Zoey was glad of the distraction.

'This stuff looks weird,' Skye said. 'It looks like one of my ice creams gone wrong.'

'I know,' Noah said, 'I'm not sure this snowball fight is going to be that effective. But it's too late to cancel things now. People will be disappointed. I better go and start the proceedings.'

He walked off just as another woman approached, who must have been Skye's sister Clover as they looked almost identical.

'Is Pearl OK?' Angel asked.

Clover nodded. 'She's fast asleep.'

Noah's voice came over the microphone. 'Ladies and gentlemen, welcome to the Sapphire Bay Hotel and to the Great Big Snowball Fight.'

There was a polite round of applause.

'Just a few rules to start with, no stones in the snowballs. We definitely don't want any injuries today, let's keep the fun nice and clean. No yellow snow either.'

The crowd laughed.

'This stuff can get quite slippery, if you fall or get knocked down, then you're out. Let's see who is the last man or woman standing. Let's do a countdown and get this thing started. Ten, nine...'

'Are we fighting against each other or with each other?' Kit asked. 'Do you want to be on my team?'

Zoey grinned. 'I think I definitely want to be on your team. You have rower's arms, so I imagine you're going to have a good throw. Plus I think we make a great team.'

Kit smiled. 'I do too.'

'... two, one, GO!' Noah said.

Suddenly all hell broke loose. Snowballs were being thrown in every direction – people had clearly already made a few of them in preparation but Zoey and Kit hadn't thought to do so. As they both ducked down to make the balls, snowballs were already flying over their heads.

Zoey scooped some of the powdered snow into her hands and immediately noticed how sticky and gloopy the mixture was, although it did make quite effective snowballs very easily. She made a small pile of them and then stood up armed to attack and got a snowball hard in her face. She laughed, wiping the gloop from her eyes, and looked round for her attacker, but there were so many snowballs flying in every direction it was impossible to see who had aimed it at her, if they had done so deliberately.

Kit was throwing balls in random directions with no real targets, which seemed like a good way to start – she didn't know anyone to deliberately aim at them. But before she could launch hers she got another snowball in the side of her head. She turned and looked and saw three teenage boys who were firing snowballs at anyone and everyone like some kind of semi-automatic weapon. Then suddenly she recognised them, these were the same boys who barged into her at the marketplace, causing her to spill scalding hot glögi over herself a few days before.

She immediately took aim and started throwing her sticky missiles at them. She hit one in the chest, the second boy on his leg and the third boy got it square in the face and then let out a satisfying wail.

Realising they were the victims of a targeted attack, all three started aiming their snowballs at her.

Kit, realising she was under siege, came to her aid, throwing snowballs that hit their target every single time, mainly the boys' faces and heads.

'Is there any reason we're attacking a group of children?' Kit said, while he refilled his arms with his ammo.

'Those are the little sods that barged into me the other day and nearly gave me third-degree burns.'

Kit laughed. 'Well, in that case…'

He doubled his efforts, throwing hard and fast, but the boys were equally fast and Zoey was hit several times in the head and chest with the snowballs. The good thing about these weird fake snowballs was they didn't hurt when they made impact, but they didn't fall off or melt like normal snowballs, they just seemed to cling to her hair and clothes.

'Actually, I think I should be thanking them,' Kit said, although he didn't stop his deluge. 'Without them, we'd never have met.'

'Oh, I think we would. I was coming to you to buy churros anyway.'

'Yes, but then you'd have been just another paying customer, one I thought was beautiful but I certainly wouldn't have plucked up the courage to ask you out. You'd have bought your churros and then gone on your way. We might not even be friends, let alone… upgraded.'

She smiled at that term.

It was funny to think that a brief moment in time had changed everything. Kit was right, if it hadn't been for the spilt glögi, they might not even know each other and now she was thinking about a future with him.

'Actually, when you put it like that, maybe we shouldn't be picking on them after all.' She turned to pick another target but the boys were hell-bent on revenge now, throwing snowball after snowball, mostly at her.

'Oh sod it,' Zoey said, bending over to refill her arsenal but the ground was slippery and, as she took three snow-balls to her head and chest, she lost her footing and tumbled to the ground.

The boys took great pleasure in this, cheering, laughing and high-fiving each other.

Kit offered out his hand to help her up but she couldn't get enough traction on the floor and, as she heaved herself up using Kit's help, he fell to the floor too. The boys' cheering went up an octave and then they quickly found another target.

'Well, I guess we're out,' Kit said, clambering to all fours and pushing himself up to his feet. He offered out his hand again to pull her up and she manoeuvred herself onto her knees then hauled herself up using his help.

She looked down at herself. The white mixture was all over her, it was in her hair, her face, all over her clothes and shoes. Kit wasn't much better.

'I don't think this stuff is going to come off easily,' Zoey said, holding out a strand of hair. It was matted with the fake snow.

'Come up to my hotel room, you can use my shower,' Kit said.

'Good idea,' Zoey said.

They'd had the foresight to take their coats off before the snowball fight had started so they collected them from a nearby bench and made their way back into the hotel. Zoey could see some of the other guests who had been in the snowball fight had already walked through reception; there were gooey sticky footprints across the shiny marble floor, up the stairs and in the direction of the lift.

'I think Noah is going to regret that snowball fight, there's going to be one hell of a clean-up operation out there and in here,' Kit said.

'I know, it's such a mess.'

They got the lift up to Kit's room and, when they walked in, she could see the dazzling view over the sea. The sun had set long ago, but she could see the moon reflected brightly in the twinkling water.

'What a great room,' Zoey said.

'I know, it really is. The bathroom is bigger than my house.'

Zoey peered round to see that the bathroom was almost as big as the bedroom.

'Please, help yourself to the shower,' Kit said.

'Actually, I think I'm going to need some help getting this stuff out of my hair,' Zoey said. 'Would you mind giving me a hand?'

'Oh sure.'

She took off her shoes and then stepped into the shower fully clothed, at least she could rinse her clothes off at the same time. She turned the shower on and let the water soak her. Kit pulled off his jumper and stepped inside the walk-in shower with her. The cubicle was huge so there was plenty of room. She turned round so her back was towards him and he started running his fingers through her hair.

The movement was so innocent but so intimate it made her breath catch in her throat. He squirted some shampoo into his hands and began massaging her hair.

Zoey closed her eyes. This shouldn't feel as good as it did and he had no idea that she was in heaven right now as he caressed her head and hair.

'The shampoo is shifting it, but it might take a while to get it all out,' Kit said.

'That's OK,' Zoey said and was embarrassed to hear how strangled her voice sounded.

His hands paused in their work. Christ, he'd heard it too.

He resumed washing her hair, working his fingers through the lengths of it, and Zoey was aware of his every touch, every nerve in her body wakening, fizzing with excitement. Marika's words echoed in her head. *Enjoy the now.*

She turned round to face him, his eyes locking with hers, and she knew he'd been enjoying that almost as much as she had.

Without a word, she leaned up and kissed him and he immediately kissed her back. God, that need for him ripped through her so fast it took her breath away. She pressed herself against him tighter and he moaned softly against her lips.

The kiss was urgent and desperate but Kit didn't try to take it any further and she liked that, although she was in the mood for something more than just a kiss.

She slid her hands underneath his t-shirt, caressing the muscles in his back. His skin was velvety soft but she could feel the hardness underneath. She moved her hands down to the hem and pulled it off in one swift movement. When his mouth returned to hers, she could feel his breath was shaky. She stroked across his shoulders and then caressed her hands over his chest and down to his stomach.

Zoey undid his jeans and then pushed them down his legs. He stepped back briefly to wriggle out of them before shuffling her back against the wall of the shower, kissing her hard. He dragged her sweater dress up over her head, taking her t-shirt with it and dumped them both on the floor of the shower. He returned his hands to her body, stroking round her back and quickly removing her bra before filling his hands with her breasts. She gasped against his lips.

He moved his hands to the waistband of her leggings and clarity filled her mind. She stopped him with a hand on his chest.

'Wait.'

'Yes, sorry,' Kit said.

'No, don't apologise, just… before this goes any further, please tell me you have some condoms?'

'I do.'

'Thank god.'

She kissed him again and then the rest of their clothes

were removed very quickly. She loved the idea of shower sex, him taking her hard and fast against the shower wall, but Kit didn't seem to be in any hurry, exploring her body with the gentlest of touches as if he was trying to commit her to memory. His hands on her skin were driving her to the point of insanity and he'd barely touched her anywhere that could be considered intimate. He traced his fingers down her arms, her back, a featherlight caress across her collar bone, nowhere where she needed him to be, but still that feeling was bubbling underneath the surface as if she was just teetering on the edge. Sex had never been like this. When she'd been with David, it had been a desperate need for each other that had been finished very quickly. Kit was very happy taking his time and she loved it, but Christ she needed more. She tried to distract herself with focussing on touching his body rather than what he was doing to her but soon her hands, which were gently caressing his back, turned to desperate claws.

'Kit, please,' Zoey begged and he smiled against her lips as if he knew exactly what he was doing to her.

She nearly wept with relief when he slipped his hand between her legs and she cried out when he touched her in the exact spot that made her go weak in the knees.

He dropped his mouth to her shoulder and then lower across her chest before taking her breast in his mouth while his fingers worked their magic. That feeling exploded through her so she was shouting out all manner of words and noises that didn't make sense. She sagged against the wall, her head leaning back on the tiles as she tried to catch her breath. He straightened, cupped her face and kissed her.

After a moment, he lifted her and she wrapped her arms and legs around him. He turned the shower off and walked out the cubicle as he continued to kiss her. He paused for a moment while he rooted in his soap bag and she liked his optimism in grabbing a handful of condoms. Then he carried her into the bedroom, laying her down on the bed with his strong body pinning her to the mattress.

'I'll get your sheets wet,' Zoey said against his lips; her hair was soaking.

'I don't care,' Kit said and then kissed her again.

The kiss seemed to go on for a while but she didn't care. She was sated now, happy. With an orgasm that powerful, she was unlikely to have another so he could do whatever he wanted with her now.

He pulled away for a second to put the condom on and then he was leaning back over her, with his eyes locked on hers, he was suddenly inside her, making her moan with a sudden desperate need again. Impossibly, that feeling started building inside her almost immediately.

'Kit.' His name was no more than a whisper on her lips.

He kissed her hard and she wrapped her legs around him, clinging to his shoulders.

As that feeling in her body continued to intensify, taking her higher and higher, he pulled back slightly to stare at her in absolute wonder. It was that look of adoration that sent her roaring over the edge and, as she fell, she took him with her.

Kit finished off the mince pie waffle, licking the brandy ice cream off his spoon. They were sitting on his bed, wrapped in the hotel bathrobes, polishing off the room service meal they'd ordered. Having amazing sex had worked up an appetite for them both. He looked at Zoey who was licking her fingers and that simple innocent act made a kick of desire slam into his gut.

She caught him looking and smiled. 'That was delicious.'

He cleared his throat. 'This night just keeps getting better and better. Great food, wonderful company, incredible sex.'

She giggled and shifted her plate to the bedside drawers and, as he did the same, she cuddled up next to him. He kissed her on the forehead.

'You look happy,' Kit said.

After making love to her, he'd waited for the doubt to come creeping in, his insecurities that made him worry she hadn't enjoyed it as much as he had. But there'd been none of that. It had been very obvious that she had enjoyed it. Afterwards, she'd cuddled up against him and given a big sigh of complete and utter contentment. And then she'd stayed there, sprawled across his chest for the longest time, instead of getting up and doing something else like Lily always had. He could have held her there forever.

'I am happy,' Zoey said, the biggest grin on her face. She looked up at him and frowned slightly. 'Are you?'

He nearly laughed out loud at that. Happy didn't even begin to cover what he was feeling right now.

'Zoey, from the moment you walked into my life, my

169

world has changed beyond recognition. The last few days have been the happiest of my life.'

She stared at him for a moment and he cursed that he'd said that. It was way too much too soon.

'I feel the same. It's ridiculous how perfect things are going. I keep waiting for it to all come tumbling down but it doesn't, it just gets better.'

He stared at her, a smile stretching across his face. He wanted to tell her he was pretty sure he was falling in love with her but it was definitely too soon for that. But a look passed between them that seemed to say it all.

'Do you think you'll get married again?' Zoey asked.

He couldn't help smiling because any other man who'd had one date and slept with a woman for the first time would be running a mile if the woman mentioned marriage, but he wasn't scared of that. Lindsey had warned him that he should slow down and not to rush into anything but he honestly could picture forever with Zoey.

'My relationship with Lily didn't put me off marriage. It dented my confidence – well, destroyed it if I'm honest. And I wondered if there was a woman out there that would want forever with me. If I found one who did who I loved I would absolutely marry again. I want the cliché: marriage, kids, a couple of dogs and a donkey. Hopefully one day I'll get it.'

'Are donkeys part of the cliché?'

'They should be. What about you? You were engaged to be married when your fiancé cheated on you. Would you go through that again?'

'The cheating part? I'd rather not. But the engaged part? Yes, I would. Like you I want the fairytale, I want the happy ever after with the man I love and our children. My bad luck in the past doesn't stop me hoping for that in the future. He'd have to be someone special,' Zoey said, trailing a finger across his chest. 'And be amazing in bed.'

'Those are pretty simple requirements.'

She giggled. 'Actually, I think that finding someone who is amazing in bed is pretty hard. I've had quite a lot of good sex in my life, some bad but mostly good. But after tonight… Well, you've set the bar impossibly high. I think you've ruined me for other men. If things don't work out for us I'll probably end up a spinster for the rest of my life as I couldn't go back to good sex after sampling the best. No pressure or anything.'

He laughed and then frowned. 'Are you seriously saying that tonight was the best sex you've ever had?'

She looked up at him and grinned. 'It was… phenomenal.'

Christ. Every single doubt and worry suddenly vanished.

'In fact, I wouldn't mind a round two, just to check,' Zoey said, kneeling up and straddling him, but frustratingly there was a sheet still between them.

He undid her robe and gently pushed it off her so he could enjoy her body in all its glory. He ran his hands over her breasts and she let out a soft moan. He leaned forward, brushing her hair off her shoulders, and then placed a gentle kiss on her throat.

'Kit, I need to tell you something.'

'What's that?' He placed a kiss on her bare shoulder.

'I like donkeys too.'

He couldn't help smiling against her skin.

CHAPTER 10

22 DECEMBER

'I brought you some fresh joulutorttu,' Marika said, standing at the entrance to Zoey's hut.

Zoey put down a scarf she was trying and failing to artfully arrange in the cabinet and eagerly moved towards her friend. She'd had breakfast in the hotel with Kit that morning but she was still hungry, especially for something sweet.

As Zoey reached out for the tart, Marika held it away from her. 'This isn't free.'

'Oh, of course. Let me get my purse,' Zoey said.

'No, you silly woman. I give you this, I want *all* the gossip. I saw Kit walking you to work this morning, you were both holding hands and staring at each other with big goofy grins. I need to live vicariously through you.'

Zoey smiled and nodded her agreement but mainly because the joulutorttu was so good. She wouldn't spill all the beans, just as in the same way she hoped Kit would be discreet too, but she could give Marika something.

Marika gave her the joulutorttu and Zoey tucked in; it tasted wonderful. 'Do you make your own jam too?'

'Yes, I tend to use blueberries and… Don't change the subject, Zoey Flynn, I'm on to you.'

Zoey laughed. 'We went to the snowball fight just like you and Elias did and we got so covered in the stuff that Kit invited me up to the room to use his shower.'

'I bet he did,' Marika waggled her eyebrows at her.

'Kit is a complete gentleman, I'm sure that the invitation was perfectly innocent,' Zoey said.

'And did it stay innocent?' Marika said.

Zoey laughed. 'Well, I needed help washing that gunky snow out of my hair.'

'I bet you did,' Marika said, practically leaning forward.

'And… one thing led to another.'

Marika squealed with excitement.

'What about you and Elias? I saw you two together before the snowball fight.'

'We got covered in the stuff too, but as we are both in the hotel we didn't need to share a shower. Although I wish I had thought of that. Then he took me out on a date.'

'Oh my god, that's amazing,' Zoey said.

'Yes it *was*. We went to that Italian place, everything was lovely and then he obviously ate something he was allergic to because he then spent most of the rest of the night in the toilet, throwing up.'

'Oh no, is he OK?'

'Yes, I think so. He texted me this morning to say he probably wouldn't be at the market today but that he had at least stopped being sick.'

'Oh, the poor thing. Food poisoning is the worst.'

'Yeah, I know, I felt so bad for him. I walked him back to his room to make sure he was OK, but needless to say there was no amazing first kiss or incredible sex for us.'

'That's such a shame. But at least you two went out on a date, that's a start, right?'

Marika nodded. 'It's nice. I like him. But it looks to me that you and Kit are head over heels in love.'

Zoey couldn't help the smile from spreading across her face.

'I know it's ridiculous, I've only known him for a few days, but everything is so perfect between us right now that it kind of feels like…' Zoey trailed off. It *was* ridiculous to be thinking of forever. There was so much more she needed to know about him before she could really consider a future.

'It's OK to fall in love,' Marika said gently. 'There's no greater feeling in the world than falling in love, why shouldn't we enjoy that moment when it comes? But try not to think too much of a future. Not yet at least. If you imagine marriage, babies, a cottage by the sea then you'll be even more disappointed if it comes to an end because not only did you lose the man you love, but you lost that bright and happy future too.'

'I totally get that. And I rushed into being engaged with my last boyfriend which ended badly. I need to go into this with a bit of caution.'

'Just enjoy what you're having with Kit right now. The other stuff will come later.'

Zoey nodded.

'And if you want a guarantee for love, you should both come along to my cookie workshop this afternoon. We'll be decorating special gingerbread cookies called piparkakut. Legend says that if you decorate a piparkakut for your loved one, you'll have everlasting love.'

'Really?'

'No, I totally made that up. But I'd love it if there were a few friendly faces there for moral support. I don't think I can count on Elias to even make it out of his hotel room today.'

'I'll be there and I'll ask Kit to come too. And you can always make a piparkakut for Elias and take it to his room tonight.'

'Oh, that's a great idea.'

Zoey's phone rang later that morning and she smiled when she saw it was Lulu calling. She obviously had some kind of sixth sense that the friendship had suddenly escalated.

'Hey Lulu, how's things with you?' Zoey said, trying to cut her off at the pass.

'All good here. Mia is teething so as you can imagine that's a wonderful and happy time where we are all getting loads of sleep,' Lulu said.

Zoey grinned.

'She's actually asleep now so I thought I would use that time to live my life vicariously through you. I love my husband, I love married life and being a mum, but I need something exciting beyond the joy of teething and potty training.'

'Ouch, double whammy.'

'Yes, Ethan has pooed pretty much everywhere except

in the potty, so yeah, we're having a great time here. Tell me something exciting and happy, I'll take anything.'

Zoey smiled. 'Well, me and Kit have upgraded our relationship.'

Lulu gasped. 'What kind of upgrade?'

'The intimate kind.'

'Oh my god,' Lulu squealed. 'That's fantastic. What was it like?'

'Incredible. Magnificent. Best sex I've ever had.'

'Good lord, that sounds like a very amazing upgrade. So are you two just doing the friends-with-benefits thing, or are you dating or should I start looking for a wedding hat?'

Zoey laughed. 'It's been one night so I don't think you'll need the wedding hat just yet but this feels like something special for us. I'm falling for him. And yes, I know I've only known him for such a short amount of time and I know that I rushed into things with David and that turned out terribly but—'

'You don't need to justify yourself to me,' Lulu said. 'You know your own mind and your heart. You can't help the way you feel. And he must be someone special if he makes you feel this way. Enjoy it. What was that quote from Tennyson? "It's better to have loved and lost than never to have loved at all." If it all goes wrong, it's better to experience the highs of falling in love than to hide yourself away for the rest of your life. If you're happy then I couldn't be happier.'

Zoey smiled. 'Thank you. I've also put a deposit down to rent a cottage here starting in January. It's a lovely little thing overlooking the harbour, and it has a large garden so

I'm going to be in my element. Mum is over the moon that I'm staying here.'

'Sounds wonderful, I can't wait to see it.'

'I can't wait for you to see it and to meet Kit.'

'I look forward to it. I'll bring the kids, they'll enjoy a trip to the beach. Maybe I'll wait until Ethan has learned how to use a toilet first.'

Zoey laughed.

'If I don't speak to you before, hope you have a spectacular Christmas with your beloved,' Lulu said.

Zoey smiled. 'And you.'

'I better go, Mia has just woken up. I love you kid.'

'I love you too.'

Zoey hung up and let out a happy sigh. She had a feeling Christmas was definitely going to be a good one.

Kit hurried through the marketplace, hoping he wasn't going to be late for the cookie-decorating workshop. It wasn't really his thing but any time spent with Zoey was definitely his thing. Lindsey was so excited that he was dating again and it was going well that she'd practically pushed him out the door when he'd told her he wanted to take an hour off and the reason why.

There were a few people milling around Marika's hut when he arrived but it was clear the cookie decorating hadn't started yet. He could see Marika was collecting money for the workshop. Nix and Lyra, the events managers at the hotel, had asked many of the stall holders to run some workshops and they'd all been told they could charge a pound per person for the workshops or two pounds if the customers got to take away a finished product. It brought in a bit of extra cash but also got people interested in their wares too.

Zoey was waiting for him outside her own hut and he couldn't help but smile when he saw her. She leaned up and kissed him when he drew near.

'Hello, you,' she said. 'Thank you for coming.'

'Well, I love cookies so it was hard to say no to,' Kit teased. 'Plus seeing you is an added bonus.'

He eyed her paintings inside her shop. It was the first time he'd seen them. She had a wonderful talent but it was hard to escape how similar they were to his dad's. There were lots of things about them that were definitely her style, but there were also a lot of parallels too.

He picked up one of the nearest ones; he loved the little comedic features. The more you stared at it, the more you saw.

'These are wonderful,' Kit said.

'Thank you.'

'They remind me of Jack Ashley's work. Have you heard of him?'

She cleared her throat. 'Yes, I have.'

'OK, ladies and gentlemen,' Marika called. 'If you'd like to gather in, that's it, squeeze round the sides. I'll do a demonstration to show you how we decorate the piparkakut, the gingerbread cookies, and then you can all have a go yourselves.'

Zoey grabbed Kit's hand and moved into the hut so they had a good view of what Marika was doing.

Kit frowned slightly. Had Zoey looked a bit guilty when

he mentioned his dad's name? There'd been a definite expression of alarm. He wondered if she'd thought he was accusing her of copying him which wasn't the case at all; he could see the styles were different. But she had seemed worried when he'd said the name Jack Ashley. He didn't make a habit of telling people who his dad was. Not because he was ashamed of him, far from it. He was incredibly proud of his dad's paintings. It was more that when he told people who his dad was their eyes would light up at this connection to this talented, well-loved man. Then when Kit told them he made his living from drawing cartoon strips, he could almost see the disappointment in their eyes. He loved his job but it was a far cry from what the great Jack Ashley used to do.

Except Zoey hadn't looked at him with disappointment when he'd told her about his job. She had been really interested in his work and he liked that.

Maybe the parallels between Zoey and his dad had been drawn before and she didn't like being compared to him, just as in the same way he hadn't liked people comparing his work unfavourably to his dad's.

'So these are our standard gingerbread cookies,' Marika said, showcasing some round scalloped biscuits. 'Although the gingerbread cookies come in all shape and sizes – we might have reindeer or Christmas trees – I like to keep to a plain shape and add decorations. You could do something simple like a snowflake.'

Marika iced three simple lines that joined up to make a six-point star and then added blobs on the end of each line. She made it look very easy and effective.

'For the icing I use powdered sugar and milk and a

really thin nozzle on the piping bag to do fine detail in the decorations,' Marika said.

She went on to demonstrate several other patterns and designs and then it was time for them to do their own.

Marika had set out tables and benches along the walls so there was enough room for everyone and Kit sat down next to Zoey. After Marika had been round to make sure everyone was OK and had passed out small ingredient cards for how to make the gingerbread cookies, they got to work.

'Why did you look so alarmed when I mentioned Jack Ashley's name?' Kit said, as he piped a small Christmas tree onto one of his cookies.

'I didn't,' Zoey said, way too quickly.

Something was going on here.

An elderly lady dressed in a fabulous velvet green cloak was sitting opposite them and she looked up at the mention of Jack Ashley's name. It was something that happened quite a lot; people still loved him. In America he had quite the cult following, there were even bobble heads and socks with his picture on. Kit clearly couldn't talk about Jack being his dad now.

'I'm afraid that might be my fault,' the elderly lady said. She leaned forward and offered out her hand to shake. 'Sylvia O'Hare. I was in Zoey's hut the other day and I was going on and on about Jack Ashley and his paintings. I'm sure Zoey here was fed up of hearing his name by the time I left. And no artist wants to be compared to another artist, even if it's favourably – we all like to think we are unique.'

Kit turned to Zoey. 'Did I offend you by suggesting your paintings remind me of Jack Ashley?'

'No,' Zoey frowned. 'Jack's art was wonderful and I wouldn't be where I am today if it wasn't for him.'

Now Sylvia looked alarmed. 'Oh, I'm sure she didn't mean anything untoward by that, just that she was inspired by him, that's all. We take our inspiration from everywhere. As a writer I'm inspired by a conversation I might overhear on the train, or something that happens in a TV programme or film. I'm sure Jack with his little TV show has inspired lots of people.'

Why did it feel like Sylvia was now trying to cover up for something? Zoey was looking really uncomfortable too. What the hell was going on?

Zoey glanced at him and Kit could see she was worried.

'Look Sylvia, I appreciate your help but you're making Kit think all sorts of things which are simply not true.' Zoey turned to him. 'I was inspired heavily by Jack and, while speaking with Sylvia the other day, I think she started putting two and two together and making five and now she's trying to cover for me when there is no need. I was concerned when you mentioned his name before that you might start to draw the same conclusions that Sylvia did.'

'And what conclusions are those?' Kit said.

He knew he needed to temper his reaction to this. Neither of them knew that Jack was his dad but he was getting an increasingly uneasy feeling about all of this. He was confused by Zoey's reaction before, now he was downright worried and he couldn't put his finger on why. If she had simply been inspired by his dad then why was she looking guilty and worried, and what exactly was

Sylvia trying to cover up? Did Zoey know something about his dad that she wasn't letting on?

Zoey took his hand underneath the table, entwining his fingers with her own. 'This is becoming a much bigger thing than it needs to be. Let's not see problems where there aren't any.'

She was right. Things were going so well between them, he didn't need to create drama. So what if she was inspired by his dad? Thousands of people had tuned into his TV series each week to watch him paint, he had probably inspired an entire generation of painters. It wasn't a big deal. Although he couldn't push the feeling away that something wasn't right.

Zoey looked at him hopefully and Kit nodded. The huge sigh of relief from Zoey did nothing to dispel his worries. He needed to talk to her about this but now was clearly not the time.

'Marika says, if you want luck in love, then we are to ice a cookie and give it to each other,' Zoey said, clearly changing the subject.

'What a lovely idea,' Sylvia said, evidently pleased the conversation had moved on. 'I'm on husband number six and I never gave Finnish cookies to any of my ex-husbands. Maybe I should have done and then we'd have had more luck. Although, I don't think I'd have wanted to have stayed married to any of my exes.'

'Maybe you can give one of these to your current husband,' Zoey suggested.

'Now that's a good idea,' Sylvia said.

Zoey started icing something onto her cookie and Kit

tried to focus on his but his mind was still replaying what Zoey and Sylvia had just been talking about.

'Are you done?' Zoey said after a while, carefully shielding her cookie.

'Yes.' He glanced across at Sylvia, who was now busily creating her own cookie. 'I made you a star, because you bring light into my life.'

Zoey smiled, looking at him with complete love in her eyes.

She passed him the cookie she had made for him and he could quite clearly see it was a donkey.

He felt a lump in his throat and leaned forward to kiss her, firmly pushing any worries about his dad out of his mind.

Kit came up as Zoey was locking up and her heart filled at the sight of him. She was falling for this man so fast that she should have been scared by it, but she wasn't, not one bit.

The conversation had got a bit worrying while they'd been making cookies that afternoon but Kit seemed to have let it go. He hadn't mentioned it at all after. And her past with Jack Ashley had no impact on him whatsoever, so she didn't feel bad about keeping her secret.

'Hey, I bought you something,' Zoey said, fishing in her bag.

He dodged a kid on a bike and stepped up in front of her. 'You have?'

She pulled out the small tub she'd bought from the toy stand a few hours before.

He frowned in confusion. 'What is it?'

'Putty.'

His eyes snapped up to hers. She'd wondered if he would get the significance of it but he definitely did.

He stepped closer, cupped her face and kissed her. There was no holding back with this kiss – every touch of his lips, his tongue, was a dark promise of what he wanted to do to her later that evening when they were alone. The memory of the night before was seared on her brain and the thought of that made her go white hot with need. She didn't want to wait until later that night.

As he moved his mouth to her throat, she fumbled with the key in the door behind her, opened it and tugged him inside. He kicked the door closed, plunging them into darkness, and he gathered her against him, kissing her hard. She pushed his coat off him and then dragged his t-shirt and jumper off in one go. As he returned his mouth to hers, she let her hands explore his bare chest and shoulders, feeling her way across his muscles in the dark. He was so strong and hard, something she hadn't fully appreciated when they'd first met. It had come as something of a surprise the night before. She teased her hands down his back and then round the front, grazing the top of his trousers, which caused him to let out a soft moan against her lips.

He shuffled her backwards, his hands snaking down her sides and then dragging her jumper dress up over her head. They slammed into the wall and one of the pictures fell to the floor. She giggled against his lips. Her bra came off and he filled his hands with her breasts. She gasped with need for him and shuffled him towards the back of the shop where there was at least a sofa, kicking her boots off and wriggling out of her leggings as the kiss continued. They banged against the counter and she heard something heavy fall out the other side. As thrilling as sex in the dark would be, they needed some light in here to see what they were doing and before they damaged any more of her stock. She fumbled around behind her and flicked on a set of battery-operated fairy lights, which at least gave a dim glow to the place and let her see Kit's wonderful body and his eyes, dark with need as they roamed across her flesh.

He moved back to kissing her again before trailing his mouth down her body. He came to the waistband of her knickers and he started slowly pulling them down, kissing her legs as he knelt to remove them completely. With his eyes locked on hers, he began kissing slowly back up her legs. Her heart was slamming against her chest, desire ripping through her as he kissed her at the top of her legs. She let out a noise that was somewhere between a scream and moan and she clamped her mouth shut in case someone outside heard her. The market would be mostly empty at this time but there might be a few people outside locking up their huts. She gripped the counter behind her hard as he continued to kiss her and touch her. Little tingles in every part of her body were suddenly turning into huge fireworks, exploding through her with such force that she suddenly found herself shouting out all manner of noises, not caring that anyone could hear, not thinking of anything but the incredible sensations ripping through her body.

Kit stood back up and she leaned against him for a moment, trying to catch her breath, her whole body trembling. To her surprise, he wrapped his arms around her and just held her against him, stroking her hair with one hand, caressing gently down her back with the other. It was so tender and so not what she was expecting after the passion and urgency of the past few minutes. Sex with David had always been fast and urgent, foreplay was rushed to get to the main event as quickly as possible. They had never cuddled halfway through. She had just had the best orgasm of her entire life and she'd expected him to lift her onto the counter and take her hard and fast, but he seemed happy to just hold her. This was about giving her what she needed, not taking what he wanted. God she loved this man. And that sudden realisation made her take a shuddery heavy breath. She knew it was ridiculous to feel this way so quickly but she knew that she did, it filled her entire heart.

'You OK?' Kit asked gently.

She nodded, unable to find the words to describe what she was feeling. 'Just need a moment.'

He kissed the top of her head and then slid his hand into hers. 'Come over here.'

He tugged her to the sofa, sat down and then pulled her onto his lap. He grabbed the blanket from the back of the sofa and wrapped it round her and then carried on stroking her through the blanket. She leaned her head on his shoulder as her breath slowed, breathing him in, relishing his Christmassy scent of cinnamon, sugar and churros. She kissed his neck and then sat up so she could kiss him properly.

He pulled back slightly to look at her, stroking her face.

'Are you OK? You were shaking like a leaf.'

'I've never had an orgasm like that before. You make me feel things that I've never...' she swallowed. It was too soon to give him her heart. 'I adore you Kit Lewis. I adore your complete and utter patience, your kindness and gentleness. I adore how you make me laugh and how you make me scream in ecstasy.' He stared at her in shock and she realised she might have pushed it too far. She got up and lay down on the sofa. 'I think you better come over here and let me show you how much you mean to me.'

He grinned and stood up. He fished a condom from his pocket and passed it to her and then quickly dispensed with his jeans and shorts so he was impressively and wonderfully naked. He lay down next to her and she rolled onto her side to make room for him, taking him in her arms and kissing him.

He took the condom off her, tore his mouth from hers for a fleeting second to rip it open with his teeth and then he was kissing her again, rolling on top of her. She wrapped her arms and legs around him and he moved deep inside her. She was already so sensitive that she could feel that sensation building inside her already. He moved against her slowly, carefully, kissing her so gently, and she couldn't help that feeling of complete love surging through her again.

He pulled back slightly to look at her, frowning with concern. 'You're shaking again.'

She smiled. 'Don't worry, it's a good thing. Don't stop.'

He kissed her again as she felt her love for him fill every part of her and she knew it was her love for him that sent her soaring over the edge.

Kit lay on the sofa watching the pattern of the fairy lights dance gently across the ceiling. Zoey was lying sprawled out on top of him, as if she'd run a marathon. Her face was resting on his chest and her soft breath across his skin was utterly divine. He stroked her hair, letting the silky strands run through his fingers. He wasn't entirely sure if she was awake or not. Her eyes were closed and she hadn't said anything for the last ten minutes. Although he was quite happy to hold her in his arms until she was ready to move. He grabbed the blanket he'd wrapped her in before and pulled it over her.

Sex with Zoey was not like anything he'd ever experienced before and he had no idea why it was so different. He'd slept with several women before Lily and sex was always good. The relationships themselves always fizzled out pretty quickly but he'd always enjoyed the sex. The women he'd been with seemed to enjoy themselves too. But not once had a woman looked at him the way Zoey had when he'd made love to her. He'd never had to hold a woman after an orgasm because she was trembling so much. But it was more than that. It wasn't just her reactions to him that were different. What *he* felt was completely different too. Every touch from her, running his fingers or his mouth across her skin, felt like heaven. It was almost like, before, sex had been this muted version, like watching a TV programme about Australia in black and white compared to standing there on the white sands, swimming in the turquoise seas, hearing the thunder of the waterfalls, tasting the incredible food. For the first time in his life, he was truly experiencing what sex should be like and it was incredible.

He knew that part of that, or maybe all of it, was down to what he felt for Zoey. He had never felt for anyone what he felt for her and that scared him. Because when it inevitably came to an end, which it always did, walking away from her would hurt more than anything.

A loud gurgling noise vibrated against his stomach and Zoey giggled against his chest.

'I think we better get something to eat otherwise there'll be more of those noises,' she said, lifting her head to look at him. Her face radiated happiness and he couldn't help smiling at her.

'We can't have that.'

She smiled and climbed off him. 'I think we need some light so we can at least find all our clothes.' She walked over to the door and flicked a switch, flooding the room with light. Then she started walking around picking up random bits of clothes that were strewn about the place and putting them on.

Kit stood up and pulled on his shorts and jeans and then noticed the trail of destruction: pictures knocked over, a small pot of pens scattered across the counter, two framed pictures lying on the floor behind the counter. He bent to pick them up, turning them over as he did, and his heart immediately fell into his stomach. He stood up and set the two pictures on the counter.

These were his dad's. He recognised them instantly. It had been so long since he'd seen his dad's originals after his mum sold them all. But, more than that, these were the missing paintings. The two that his dad had taken down from the walls of his gallery shortly before he died and walked out with. No one had any idea what had happened to them, where he had taken them. Now suddenly they were here, in a Christmas market on a tiny Cornish island, hundreds of miles away from his dad's gallery. Kit felt like he'd found some lost treasure. They were wonderful – the detail of the houses, the colour of the sky, the texture of the sea. He loved the flowers; they were something none of his father's other paintings had. He'd never seen these before apart from in photos and it was incredible to have this sudden connection with his dad again after all these years.

'Oh!' Zoey said, softly, when she saw what he was looking at. She came up beside him.

'These are Jack Ashley paintings,' Kit said.

'Yes they are.'

'Originals.'

'Yes.'

'These are the missing paintings. He took them from his gallery just before he died.'

'You know a lot about them,' Zoey said.

'I should, Jack Ashley is my dad.'

He looked up and watched the colour drain out of her face. Zoey went so pale he thought she might suddenly pass out. She sat down heavily on the sofa, letting out a heavy breath.

'Are you OK?'

'Yes, I… yes,' she said, quietly, when she quite clearly wasn't. 'But you can't be his son. You're Kit Lewis, he was Mike Ashley, Jack Ashley to everyone else.'

'Mum kept her surname when she married; she was a respected non-fiction author. When we were born, Dad insisted we had her name rather than his to protect us a little from his fame.'

'Oh!' Zoey said, softly. She seemed scared and he didn't understand why.

He turned to look at the paintings.

'Where did you get these?'

She cleared her throat. 'I, umm... bought them from the internet.'

He suddenly didn't believe her and he hated that feeling, not only because he didn't like being lied to, but also because what would make Zoey lie?

'Who from?'

'I can't remember, just some guy who was selling them,' she said vaguely.

'How much did you buy them for?'

'Oh, I don't know, I... maybe a few hundred each.'

'Well you got a bargain. Dad's paintings went for between three and five thousand.'

'I... I didn't know that.'

'And these, the infamous missing paintings that mysteriously vanished, these would be worth probably double that.'

'I just saw them for sale and I quite liked them, so I bought them, I didn't question the price.'

'Let me buy them off you.' Kit pulled out his credit card. 'Let's say five thousand for the pair.'

'No.' Zoey's voice was firm. 'They're not for sale.'

'They have no meaning to you, these are important to my family,' Kit said. Now he'd found them, he had no intention of losing them.

'They do mean something to me. I'm not selling them.'

'Why do they mean something to you?' Kit said.

She stared at him and then shook her head. 'I don't feel well, I'm going to go home.'

'I thought we were going to go and get something to eat.'

'I can't. Not tonight. I feel sick.'

He grabbed his t-shirt and jumper and pulled them on. 'Well, let me walk you home.'

'I'm fine.' She stood up and grabbed her coat. He pulled on his boots and she ushered him out of the hut, turning out the lights and locking the door behind her.

'What's going on, Zoey?'

'Nothing, I'm just not feeling great. I'll see you tomorrow.'

She hurried off before he could say another word and it took him a few moments to realise that she'd gone in the opposite direction to get to her house.

He stared into the darkness, long after she'd disappeared, wondering what the hell had just happened.

Zoey let herself into her mum's house and called out for her mum. Beth stuck her head out from the kitchen and Zoey saw her face light up into a big smile and then crumple in concern.

'Zoey, what's happened?'

She felt tears prick her eyes as she stepped inside and closed the door behind her. She couldn't believe this was happening. Of all the people in the world that she could fall in love with, why did it have to be Mike's son? Life was spectacularly unfair.

Zoey took a deep breath. 'I've fallen in love with Kit.'

'Oh that's wonderful,' her mum almost whooped with delight.

'Don't,' Zoey said. 'Don't get excited. He's Mike's son.'

Beth's face fell.

Zoey walked into the lounge, dumping her coat over the arm of the chair, and her mum followed her in.

'Are you sure?'

'He found Mike's paintings in my hut and he told me they were his dad's.'

'Oh,' Beth said and then was quiet for a moment. 'Did you tell him?'

'Of course I didn't,' Zoey said. 'Mike didn't want anyone to know. If this gets out it could ruin Mike's memory and people's opinion of him.'

Zoey sighed as she sat down.

Her mum sat down next to her.

'I can't tell him. Not only because I wouldn't want to betray Mike but because I just don't know how Kit will take it. I think he'll be hurt his dad never told him and I don't want to be the one to ruin that memory of his dad. Kit adored Mike, his dad was his hero. It would kill me to do anything to hurt him. But I also can't lie to him. I've already lied to him today when he asked me where I got the paintings from and I hate that.'

Beth was silent for a moment. 'OK, it doesn't need to be a big deal. So he found Mike's paintings in your hut, it doesn't mean anything. Tell him the truth. Tell him we were neighbours and he gave you the paintings.'

'Except he already knows something is up. I completely freaked out when he saw them and I found out who he was. All I could think about was Kit finding out the truth. And it is a big deal. I love this man so much I can already see a forever with him. But how would that ever work? I'd have to lie to him for the rest of my life. Except, in reality, no one can keep a secret for that long. At some point, I'd trip up or you would. We'd say something seemingly innocent and he'd connect the dots. One day he would find out and how would he feel then that I'd lied to him for so long? How can we have any kind of future if I can't be honest with him?'

Zoey felt a tear fall down her cheek at the thought she might have to end things with Kit when everything was so utterly perfect. That didn't seem fair.

'OK, so maybe we tell him, maybe it's time he knew,' Beth said.

'Mike took that secret with him to the grave. He knew he was dying and he never told his family. Why should we change that now?'

'Mike never expected you and Kit to fall in love, that changes everything. He wouldn't want his secret to be kept at the expense of his son's happiness.'

'But Kit won't be happy to find this out, will he? Don't you think he might see his dad as less and I'd hate for that to happen.'

Zoey felt more tears fall down her cheeks. There was no solution to this that would end in a happy ever after for them.

CHAPTER 11

Kit was waiting for Zoey the next day outside her hut and she still had no idea what she was going to say to him. But if she couldn't lie to him and she couldn't tell him the truth, where did that leave them? One day he would find out the truth and then hate her for the deceit.

'Hey, are you feeling better?' Kit asked.

She swallowed down the lump of emotion in her throat. 'Not really.'

'Look, I'm really sorry if I upset you yesterday about those paintings. It was such a shock to see them, they've been missing for so long and then suddenly they were here. It threw me.'

She opened the door and pushed open the hatch to let in the world. Then she went to the back of the shop and carefully stacked Mike's paintings back under the counter so they wouldn't have to look at them.

Kit watched her. 'Although, I'm not totally sure about your reaction to it. Want to explain to me what's going on?'

Her mouth was dry and she had no words to fill it. She

195

stared at him for the longest time, his lovely face, his patient eyes. There was nothing she could say or do that would make this situation better.

'How do you feel about secrets?' Zoey said, eventually.

Kit frowned. 'I can't say I'm a fan. Real relationships, the ones that work, are honest and open. We talked about this before, you said secrets lead to lies and distrust.'

'Well yes, but I meant affairs, problems in the relationship. This doesn't have anything to do with us.'

'Honesty is important, about everything.'

Zoey felt tears smarting her eyes and shook her head. 'I'd have to agree.'

'Then tell me what's going on. Why do you have my dad's paintings, why did you get so upset when you found out I'm his son?'

'I wish I could tell you Kit, I really do, but I can't.'

'Do you not trust me?'

'Of course I do.'

'But not enough to share this secret.'

'It would ruin everything and I can't do that. I can't lie to you either. You mean too much to me for that. I didn't buy these paintings off the internet, I'm sorry I lied about that. They were a gift but I can't tell you anything more, and if you care about me at all then you'll respect my privacy about this.'

He stared at her. 'I'm not sure I can let this go. If you know something about my dad then I have a right to know.'

'What if your dad didn't want you to know?' Zoey said, and instantly regretted it. She was saying too much.

'What would my dad not want me to know?'

'Kit, please,' Zoey said, softly. 'I can't do this.'

He didn't say anything for the longest time. Eventually he spoke. 'How can we move forward in our relationship if we can't be honest with each other?'

Tears filled her eyes. She couldn't lose him over this. But revealing the truth would taint everything he thought about his dad, and she just couldn't hurt Kit that way for her gain. There was also the added worry that telling him would make him push her away anyway, maybe he wouldn't believe it. And why would he, her word over that of the dad he adored? Then she wouldn't have gained anything, she would have hurt Kit and lost him too.

'I'm sorry, I really am,' Zoey said. 'But you have to trust me that you really are better off not knowing.'

He stared at her as if he didn't know her at all and then he turned and walked out.

The tears fell down her cheeks. Everything had been going so perfectly and now it felt like it was all over.

The demand for churros and crêpes changed throughout the day. People often came for crêpes for breakfast but they weren't really interested in the churros until mid to late morning when they would outsell the crêpes by a mile. Kit found himself thankful for this quiet lull this time in the morning; he really needed to talk to Lindsey about all of this. He watched her serve a customer with a Nutella and banana crêpe and waited impatiently for the customer to leave.

'So I need to tell you something,' Kit said, when the

customer was walking away, chocolate smeared over their lips. 'And I don't know if it's something or nothing but…'

'Come on out with it.'

'You know Dad's lost paintings, the two he took from the gallery just before he died? Well, Zoey has them in her hut.'

Lindsey stared at him with wide eyes. 'I think that's definitely something. Why does she have them, where did she get them?'

'She won't tell me. At first she said she bought them from the internet but then admitted that was a lie. She says they were a gift but she won't tell me who from. She had no idea I was Dad's son, that I was connected to those paintings, and when I told her she went very pale and practically ran away from me last night. She won't tell me why that upset her so much. I've asked her what's going on but she says Dad wouldn't want me to know and she can't tell me.'

'What the hell? She knew Dad?'

'I don't know, maybe. I guess. Or the person that gave her those paintings knew him. She called him Mike and only close friends and family knew him as Mike or Michael, to the rest of the world he was Jack Ashley.'

Lindsey shook her head. 'What does all this mean? Dad didn't have secrets or skeletons in the cupboard. Did he?'

Kit shrugged. 'If you asked me that yesterday I'd have said no, but now I have no idea.'

'Do you think he was having an affair?' Lindsey said.

Kit bit his lip. That thought had occurred to him too, that would explain why Zoey said his dad wouldn't want him to know. He shook his head. 'He adored Mum. They were so in love. I just can't see that he was sleeping with someone else behind her back.'

Lindsey absently stirred the crêpe mixture. 'Maybe he owed someone money and thought giving them the paintings would be the best way to pay off that debt.'

'That's possible. But I think we were doing OK, weren't we, financially? I don't remember Mum and Dad ever struggling to pay the bills. Who could he possibly owe money to and why?'

Lindsey sighed and they were silent for a while.

'I said her work was very similar to Dad's,' Lindsey said. 'That's a bit of a coincidence, isn't it, considering his paintings have turned up in her hut? She must have known him.'

Kit brushed his hand through his hair in frustration. None of this made sense.

'I can't believe those paintings are here, after all this time. Do you know how much they would be worth, the fabled missing paintings?' Lindsey said.

'We'll never find out, she refuses to sell them to me.'

'Why not? Surely we have more right to them than she does. They were our dad's. If anyone has the right to benefit from them, it should be us.'

'Zoey has the right to do what she wants with those paintings; keep them, sell them. They were a gift either directly or indirectly from our dad, but he took them from the gallery under his own free will, for his own reasons, and we have no right to interfere with that. And what would you do with them anyway if we did have them? Sell them so they can sit in someone else's house where we'd never see them again, to someone with no connection to Dad at all other than they liked his paintings? Zoey has a connection to Dad; these paintings are important to her. I'd rather see those paintings somewhere where they mean something to somebody than sell them on for a quick buck. Yes, I want to know what the connection is, why he gave them to her or someone else. For good or bad, this feels like a piece of Dad's life that we never knew about and I'd like to solve this mystery. But no matter what we find out, those paintings are hers.'

'OK, OK, I'm sorry,' Lindsey said. 'It's just that this whole thing is so odd. Why would Dad give those paintings away and not leave them for us?'

'We had eighty-three paintings, he took two for someone else – I think we got a good deal,' Kit said.

'True. We still need to find out how she ended up with them. Do you think Craig might know why Dad took them from the gallery?'

'He might.'

'He said he had something important to tell us about Dad. Do you think this is connected?' Lindsey said.

'I guess we'll ask him at lunch.'

Craig was waiting for them in the hotel restaurant when they arrived. It had been over ten years since Kit had last seen him and age had not been kind to his dad's elder brother. He'd put on a lot of weight and lost a lot of hair. His cheeks held that permanent redness of someone who enjoyed a bit too much to drink and his uneven teeth were yellowy when he smiled at them.

'Thank you for meeting me. God, you both have grown so much.'

He offered his arms out for a hug but Kit extended his hand instead. Craig paused for a moment and then shook it before shaking Lindsey's hand too. They all sat down.

They took a few moments to look through the menu and place their order and Kit couldn't help thinking that Craig seemed nervous.

The waiter went off to take their order to the kitchen and immediately Craig leaned forward to talk to them.

'I've been wanting to get in touch for so long. Me and your dad, we shouldn't have fallen out like we did and I regret that more than anything. Family is important, don't you think?'

'Depends on the family,' Kit said and then sighed when Lindsey gave him a filthy look. He'd promised to come into this meeting with an open mind and he'd failed at the first hurdle. 'Sorry. Yes, family is important. What was it you and Dad fought over?'

'Oh well, that's a bit awkward. You see, I loaned your dad some money and he never paid it back.'

Kit tutted. This meeting was clearly going to be a waste of time if Craig was going to lie to them about their dad.

Lindsey folded her arms across her chest. 'Dad was always loaning *you* money and you never paid it back.'

Craig licked his lips nervously. 'I don't think that's fair. I didn't have a job and your dad was this big rich celebrity.'

Their uncle had a long, long list of failed jobs behind him. He often walked out of jobs after having rows with his boss when he'd only been there for a few days or weeks. He reminded Kit of Del Boy in a way, with his fingers in so many pies, his dodgy dealings and his get-rich-quick schemes. Only Craig wasn't funny and likeable, there was a dark side to him. Kit was pretty sure he would sell his own granny if it made him a quick buck. Coupled with his huge gambling problem and borrowing money from dodgy people to pay his debts, he always seemed to be short of funds.

'It wasn't Dad's job to bail you out. I'm pretty sure this last argument was because you wanted more money and Dad refused,' Kit said.

'I don't think we need to get bogged down in what happened over ten years ago,' Craig said, obviously feeling like he was losing his audience. 'The important thing is we're together again. We had such lovely times when you were kids, I'd take you to the beach—'

'You'd tag along when our parents took us to the beach,' Lindsey said.

'Well, I guess, but we'd play rounders and cricket together and I'd go with you on the fairground rides.'

He looked at them both and clearly could see the scepticism.

'Me and your dad were so close when we were kids,' Craig said, obviously trying a different tack. 'We'd go everywhere together. And I was so happy for his success, he deserved it. I loved his paintings. What I wouldn't give to see them again. Do you still have them?'

'We sold them,' Kit said. 'Or rather Mum did. Almost all of the money went to a stroke charity. The rest she spent on a cruise.'

'They're gone. The money too? But you must still make

money from the sale of his prints and merchandise?' Craig was looking increasingly desperate.

Kit leaned forward. 'If you came to us for money, there is none.'

Craig stared at him. 'No, no, of course not. I just can't believe all the paintings have gone. I'm disappointed because I was so hoping to see them again.'

It was such a lie and Kit considered calling him out on it.

'There's two here in the marketplace,' Lindsey blurted out. 'Hut number nine.'

'Lindsey,' Kit said, sharply.

'What? You said you were going to ask him about them. A few weeks before Dad died he walked into his gallery and took two paintings. No one had any idea what he did with them and why and now they turn up here. Zoey, the girl who runs the hut, is a painter herself and her style is very similar to Dad's. The mystery deepens because she won't tell Kit how she came to have the paintings, and when she found out that Kit was Dad's son, she freaked out. We thought you might know something about it?'

Craig looked thoughtful for a moment and Kit cringed. He didn't want Craig to know about Zoey and the paintings. He didn't want Craig anywhere near her.

'What was it you wanted to say to us?' Lindsey said. 'You said there was something important you wanted to tell us about Dad?'

'Well, there's no easy way to say this. There was a woman,' Craig said, which had Kit sitting up in his seat. 'You know your dad had a flat in London – there was a woman that lived next door. I believe they were *friends.*'

'Are you saying Dad had an affair?' Kit asked.

'No. I don't know. Maybe.'

'Maybe they were just friends,' Lindsey said.

Craig made a face to suggest he didn't believe that. 'Men and women can't be friends.'

'Sure they can, especially when one of them is happily married,' Lindsey said.

At that point the waiter arrived with their meals and Craig happily tucked in, completely unaware of the turmoil he'd unleashed with that flippant comment. Did his dad really have an affair? The thought made Kit feel sick.

'Did Dad ever tell you he was having an affair?' Kit asked.

Craig shook his head and Kit found some small relief in that. 'No, but after his stroke something changed. I'd ask him if I could come down and visit while he was in London and he'd never let me. He was hiding something, I know he was.'

'Did Dad say anything about this woman that made you think he was having an affair?'

Craig thought about this as he chewed.

'I don't know, it was more of a gut feeling. He told me once that he had really lovely neighbours.'

Kit let out an exasperated sigh. Saying his neighbours were lovely wasn't exactly hard evidence either, neither was Craig's gut feeling.

'This woman, did she have a daughter?' Kit asked.

'You know what, I think she might have,' Craig said, clearly eager to spill the beans.

Kit didn't know what to do with this information. His

dad had adored his mum, they were always holding hands and kissing and cuddling. He couldn't believe he'd been screwing around with someone else while he was in London. But Craig was right, his dad had changed after the stroke. He'd struggled with his painting initially and had got really down about it. He'd spent more and more time away from home in the six months or so after the stroke, insisting he needed time on his own to focus on his paintings. And then he'd come back a changed man, he was happy and relaxed again. He'd never painted at home after that, insisting he did his best work in London. He'd spend an extra day down there most weeks rather than just the weekend, but he'd found something that worked for him so Kit and his family never questioned it. Had his dad really been having an affair with another woman rather than working on his paintings? And, even worse, might that woman turn out to be Zoey's mum?

Kit stared at his food, not feeling remotely hungry. He had to get to the bottom of this somehow and trusting Craig and his gut wouldn't give him the answers he needed. It was quite obvious he had come for money and could now be making up stuff about his dad just to get them on his side.

He needed to talk to Zoey and find some way to get her to tell him the truth.

It had been a long day for Zoey. She felt utterly heartbroken. She'd gone to look for Kit at lunchtime but his hut had been all closed up. Then later in the afternoon she'd popped down again but he'd had a massive queue and whether he didn't see her or didn't want to see her she didn't know, but he hadn't acknowledged her at all. It was coming to the end of the day and she had no idea whether he would come and find her again or whether she should go and seek him out. She still had no idea what she could say to him to make this right.

Zoey was standing in Marika's hut, selling off the last of Marika's cookies and tarts while Marika popped to one of the other stalls to grab something before they closed. There were quite a few people queuing for the cookies, mainly because Marika always slashed the price at this time of day.

There was a bit of commotion further down the row of huts and when she looked she could see a man dressed as Santa, carrying a large sack, walking into the huts and giving small presents to the stall holders.

Zoey smiled. The man looked like he could be Seamus, the village mayor – he had the same rotund figure and white beard as Seamus, although the beard this Santa had was definitely fake. She wondered if it was to cover Seamus's real beard and therefore conceal his identity.

She served two more customers with a small bag of cookies and watched as Santa walked down the row, 'Ho-ho-ho-ing' as he went and wishing everyone a Merry Christmas. He stopped at every stall and went inside to give the stall holders each a gift. He went into Zoey's hut, just as a mother and child came up to buy some cookies too. She took payment just as Santa left her own hut and approached her, offering out a small box. 'Merry Christmas.'

'Merry Christmas,' Zoey said, and gave him a cookie. She was sure Marika wouldn't mind. He was Santa after all.

He chuckled and went on his way, stopping at more of the stalls as he went.

Zoey stared after him. He looked so familiar. Even though she could see only his eyes and rosy cheeks, there was something about him she'd seen before, although she couldn't place her finger on where or who it was. She was pretty sure it wasn't Seamus though, as she'd originally thought.

A few minutes later, as Zoey was selling the last bag of cookies, Marika came back.

'Hey, have you been busy?'

'A bit, no one can resist half-price cookies.'

'I'm so sorry, I thought I'd only be a few minutes, but the queue at the hog roast place was huge and I was starving. I've been meaning to try their sandwiches for ages but every time I walk past the queue is big.'

'It's no bother. I sold all your cookies and we had a visit from Santa.'

'Santa Claus?'

'Yes, he was giving gifts to all the stall holders. Here's yours.'

She passed Marika the box. Marika rattled it and then eagerly opened it. Inside was a cheap plastic ring that looked like it had fallen out of a cracker.

'Hmm, nice,' Marika deadpanned.

Zoey pulled a face. 'I was looking forward to seeing my gift but now I'm not so sure.'

'Well go and have a look, maybe you got something better than me.'

'That wouldn't be hard.'

Zoey wandered into her hut but could see no box or bag or any present at all. That was weird, Santa had distinctly gone into her hut.

She moved to the back of the hut and looked around there and then came back to the counter and the bottom fell out of her world.

Both of Mike's paintings were gone.

CHAPTER 12

Kit was locking up his hut. Lindsey had left after lunch as she was going away with her boyfriend over Christmas, but he could hardly complain when he'd left her to man the hut so many times already.

He needed to talk to Zoey and he was hoping to catch her before she left but, as he looked down the row of huts, he saw her hurrying towards him. He felt his heart leap at the sight of her but then it dropped into his stomach when he realised she was crying.

He moved towards her quickly.

'Zoey, what's happened?'

'Your dad's paintings have gone, they've been stolen.'

'Shit, when?'

'Just now, no more than twenty minutes ago. There was a man dressed as Santa going into the huts and giving presents to the stall holders. I was manning Marika's stand for her and he went into my hut, I presumed to leave me a present but he took my paintings. I watched him come out and didn't think anything of it. He had this big bulging sack and he must have shoved them in there. And then he came to me and gave me a present, and I gave him a bloody free cookie and then he left. Christ, those paintings, I have to get them back.'

'And I'll help you. First things first, have you called the police?'

'Christ, no.' Zoey fumbled in her bag with shaky hands and grabbed her phone. 'I just had to come and tell you first. I can't believe it, I can't believe someone stole them.'

He checked his watch. 'I don't think Santa thought this through. No one is getting off the island at this time. It's high tide in half hour. The causeway will be covered in water right now. If we call the police they can organise a blockade for low tide.'

'Do you think they'd really do that?'

'This is art theft. Those paintings are worth around five thousand pounds each. I think the police would take that very seriously.'

A thought suddenly occurred to him. Could his uncle be behind this? Craig had come here looking for money and the fact those paintings were worth so much would be very attractive. Craig had spent his life doing dodgy things for cash – although stealing was a bit extreme, Kit certainly wouldn't put it past him. Anger filled him but he had to put that aside for a while to take care of Zoey, who was trembling and visibly upset. He watched her unlock the phone, tears falling down her cheeks.

'Hey.' He put his hands on her shoulders. 'We'll get those paintings back for you, I promise.'

She nodded, wiping the tears from her cheeks.

'Here, let me make the call.'

She sniffled and passed him the phone. He dialled the number and then slipped his arm round her shoulders as he explained the situation to the police.

He hung up and passed her back the phone. 'They are going to try and send someone over in a boat tonight to take some fingerprints and talk to us. And they will send a van down to the end of the causeway at low tide early hours in the morning. I'm guessing there won't be too many people leaving the island at that time. Let's go and talk to Noah and Aria at the hotel, my guess is that Santa is probably staying there. Maybe someone saw something.'

Half hour later Zoey was sitting in Aria's office at the hotel with a hot chocolate in her hands as Angel, Nix and Lyra scanned through the Christmas market webcams to see if they could discover anything. They'd already seen Santa walking through the market giving out presents and going into huts to deliver them. They'd even captured the moment he'd walked into Zoey's hut and then back out again a few moments later, but there was no evidence he'd taken the paintings and the webcams hadn't picked up a clear enough image of the man's face to be able to identify him. They were now trawling the footage before and after the incident to see if they could pick him up or find anything else untoward.

Kit was on one of the hotel computers, trying to set up

some kind of Google Alert to let them know if anyone tried to sell it. She wasn't totally sure how that worked and wasn't hopeful that it would. The internet was a huge place, how could you keep an eye on every corner of it?

She watched him as he tapped away on the computer. To his credit, he hadn't once brought up her connection to the paintings, although judging by her reaction to losing them, he must know now that she had a link to his dad – why else would she have got so upset? She was grateful he was willing to help her after she refused to sell him the paintings and tell him the secret. She'd been worried that he wouldn't want anything to do with her.

Aria walked into the office with Noah. 'Right, we've spoken to the hotel receptionists that have been on duty today. Tilly says she saw a man dressed as Santa a few hours ago. Could be our guy, but maybe not. The hotel is filled with the market stall holders, entertainers and regular guests and families. Any one of them could have a legitimate reason for dressing up as Santa. Tilly didn't think anything of it. Delilah, one of the other receptionists, says she saw a man dressed as Santa come back in and he was carrying a big sack, which is more useful as the first Santa sighting wasn't carrying one.'

'Any CCTV in the hotel, in the corridors or main areas?' Zoey asked.

Noah shook his head. 'It's not something we've ever needed. We're a quiet little hotel in the furthest corner of Cornwall. Art theft or any kind of theft is just not some-thing we see here. We only have the webcams set up for marketing purposes.'

'And they aren't giving us anything,' Nix said, closing

his laptop. 'This whole Santa thing was an elaborate scheme to steal the paintings. He didn't just walk in there, accidentally see them and then decide to steal them. This was all planned.'

'Maybe it wasn't,' Lyra said. 'How did this guy know they were there? Zoey said the paintings were under the counter.'

'They weren't for the first few days I was here, they were hanging on the walls,' Zoey said. 'Anyone could have seen them in those first few days and decided to come back and steal them. It was only when someone started asking questions about them that I put them away.'

'Who was asking questions?' Noah said.

'Some elderly lady called Sylvia O'Hare,' Zoey said. 'I highly doubt she has anything to do with this.'

'I can pretty much guarantee it wasn't her,' Aria said. 'She's a very regular guest in our hotel. I know her well.'

'Jack Ashley's work is so distinctive, anyone could have recognised it,' Angel said. 'And we've had hundreds if not thousands of people walking through the market since it opened.'

'I still think my uncle Craig is involved in all of this, this would be exactly the kind of thing that he would do,' Kit said.

'Why would he steal my paintings?' Zoey said.

'Because I think he came here looking for money. When we told him there was no money left in Dad's estate and all the paintings had been sold, I could see he was gutted.'

'You said he only arrived on the island today. How would he have known about the paintings?' Noah said.

'Because... we told him. Well, my sister did.'

'Why would you tell him about my paintings?' Zoey said.

'I'm sorry, I was talking to Lindsey about it. We were trying to figure out how you came to have them. You have to understand those paintings have been missing for nearly ten years and we always wondered why Dad took them from the gallery and what happened to them. For them to turn up here after all these years is wonderful and intriguing. Of course I'm going to talk about it with my sister. We were going to ask Craig if he knew why Dad took those paintings from the gallery. I didn't realise she'd blurt it out to Craig that the paintings were here.'

Zoey sighed. Maybe all this would have been avoided if she'd been semi honest with Kit, told him she was neighbours with his dad, that she'd drawn the flowers on the missing paintings. She didn't need to go into detail about his dad's secret but maybe revealing the connection would have been enough.

'It is weird that you two never met before the market and then you end up here with his dad's mystery lost paintings. How did you come to have them?' Aria asked.

Zoey felt her heart leap at the thought she would have to explain everything here in front of everyone.

'Those paintings belong to Zoey,' Kit said, firmly. 'How she came to have them has no bearing on the fact that they are currently stolen.'

'Well, it's entirely possible that your uncle did take the paintings,' Noah said. 'But I can't just barge into the man's room without some kind of evidence. Our guests have a right to privacy. If you mention your concerns to the police when they get here they may wish to question him but I can't just search a room without very good reason.'

They were silent for a moment.

'Noah's right. But there might be a way round it,' Aria said. 'We could send one of the maintenance team to his room because there's been a report on a leak and they want to see which rooms are affected. Or we send room service up with some food, compliments of the hotel, or a bottle of wine to apologise for… noise or something. There are lots of reasons we could come up with to gain access to his room. Now, if he's stashed them away in a wardrobe I think it could be tricky to have reason to search his wardrobe, but if they are just left out on the side, at least we'd see them.'

Noah smiled. 'I love your cunning side. Leave it with me.'

He walked out.

'In the meantime, I have set up multiple Google Alerts with every possible variation on the titles of those paintings and Jack Ashley's name,' Kit said. 'I've even set up alerts for Jack Ashley's missing and lost paintings. If he tries to sell them online, we'll know about it.'

'I think that's a great idea,' Angel said. 'And also something we want to encourage because the police can trace the owners of the seller's accounts, that's hard evidence. If the thief gets off the island, then the chances of those paintings disappearing are even greater. If we make it clear to all guests checking out that the police will be on the other side of the causeway checking cars that will discourage the thief from leaving, whether the police are there or not. Then they'll be forced to try and sell it online and then take it to the post office on the island to mail out. And if we get alerts that he's put it up for sale, we've got him.'

It was hard for Zoey to imagine she'd ever see those paintings again but at least there seemed to be a plan.

Zoey lay in Kit's bed and watched him as he moved around the room. He'd persuaded her to stay with him in case they got a hit in the early hours from one of the Google Alerts. She was still surprised he wanted anything to do with her. It wasn't the best start to a relationship to have all these secrets floating around between them. She was waiting for him to question her again, but so far he hadn't mentioned it.

He slipped into bed next to her and she rolled over to face him.

'Are you OK?' Kit asked gently.

She nodded.

'We'll get those paintings back for you, I promise. I still think this is Craig. I texted Lindsey about it all and she thinks it could be him too. He's too stupid to get away with it. He's certainly not some criminal mastermind. And if the police come over tomorrow morning and talk to him, he'll crumble within five seconds of questioning.'

'I think it could be him too. Noah said Craig was very cagey when he went up to his room and refused to let him in. We just need some evidence, something concrete to pin to him.'

'Agreed, and if he tries to sell it, we've got him. Let's get some rest, we might get woken up in the early hours once he realises he can't get off the island.'

He leaned forward and kissed her on the forehead.

She frowned. She'd been expecting the Spanish Inquisition. She knew she had to give him something and, while she couldn't tell him the secret she'd kept for the last fifteen years, she could tell him some of it.

'Kit, I need to tell you why these paintings are so important to me.'

He shook his head. 'You don't have to tell me anything.'

'I do. There's something I can't tell you as it's not really my secret to share and I know your dad wouldn't want you to know but I can tell you the rest.'

He stared at her, waiting for her to explain.

'I told you before about my mum's friend who moved next door. That was your dad. He moved in next to my mum when I was around nine years old and they became really good friends. Whenever he was there at weekends, they'd cook for each other, he'd come round and we'd watch movies together and he taught me to paint. We'd spend hours painting together. He was a patient, kind and wonderful man.'

Zoey paused, wondering what Kit would make of this. She was fairly sure Mike wouldn't have gone home and told his family about this little arrangement.

Kit didn't say anything so she pressed on.

'I used to love painting flowers, I'd do whole meadows filled with them. I told him once his paintings needed flowers too and he let me paint some on two of his paintings. The two he gave to me before he died. He gave them to me because they were a collaboration and I love them

217

because they remind me of the time we spent painting together when I was a child. He instilled in me a huge passion for painting and it's something I can't imagine ever not doing now.'

Finally Kit spoke. 'Wow, I had no idea. He always talked about how he wanted to teach art, but he didn't have any qualifications. He thought about teaching night classes at his local college but when he became famous he thought people would be coming to his classes for all the wrong reasons when really he just wanted to share his love of painting. I'm so pleased he got to do that with you. I can't believe, all those years those paintings hung in his gallery and no one knew that you worked on it together.'

'He added a Z to his signature. To anyone else it would have just looked like an unusual flourish, but he did it deliberately so my name was on the painting too.'

'That sounds like him,' Kit said, smiling.

She watched him. 'You're not mad?'

'No, why would I be?'

'I don't know, because your dad spent time painting with someone else?'

'I'm really not the jealous sort. I'm glad he was happy, I always used to think he'd be so bored and lonely down in London by himself. I'm glad he had friends.'

She felt relieved. There was other stuff that she wanted to tell him too, but she knew she couldn't. But at least she had told him as much as she could.

He suddenly frowned. 'Wait a minute. After his stroke, the paramedics said a young girl had saved him. That was you?'

Oh god, now she felt sick.

She swallowed the lump in her throat. 'We were painting together when it happened.'

'Oh shit, you were there?'

She paused before speaking, licking her lips as her mouth was suddenly dry. 'Kit, I always wondered if it was my fault.'

'What do you mean?'

'He'd come back from the gallery and he felt like crap. He wanted to go and have a lie-down and I pleaded with him to paint with me. I always wondered if I'd let him rest whether it would have happened at all.'

'Zoey, I'm no medical expert, but I'm pretty sure that a stroke is not caused by someone badgering someone else, or by painting. And if you'd let him rest, it's highly likely he would have died alone in his bed.'

'I'm sure you're right but I felt guilty for years.'

'Well there's no need. We were so grateful for what you did. I thought perhaps you had found him after the stoke, I didn't realise you were actually there. That must have been awful to see him like that. Were you alone?'

Zoey nodded. 'I completely freaked out, wishing I could do more.'

'You put him in the recovery position, you called an ambulance. You saved his life.'

'I didn't feel particularly heroic. Afterwards, when he was struggling to paint again, I kept thinking if only I'd done this, or I should have done that.'

'What more could you have done? There's very little you can do when someone has a stroke.'

'Yeah, I know.'

They were quiet for a while.

'Thank you for telling me.'

'Oh Kit, there's so much more I wish I could say but I can't. And this will always be hanging over our heads, you will always be wondering what I'm keeping from you and, like Sylvia, you'll start to see things that aren't there, you'll jump to the wrong conclusions. I think there will always be a little part of you that won't trust me if I can't always be completely honest with you. You'll start to think what else am I hiding from you. I don't know how we move forward after this. I can't tell you the truth, I can't lie to you, so what happens next?'

Kit let out a heavy breath. 'I keep telling myself I don't need to know, that whatever it is, it's in the past. It's been nearly ten years since Dad died, why upset the apple cart now? But this is to do with my dad, my family, *my* past. I have to know. What's more important to you, this secret you kept for my dad when you were a child or us?'

'Kit, that's not fair. Your dad wouldn't want you to know. What's more important to you, a fifteen-year-old secret or us?'

He stared at her for the longest time. 'I think you're right, this secret will always be there between us. I will do everything I can to help you get those paintings back but after that I think we need to draw a line under us before it goes any further.'

Zoey heard the sob escape her throat but she'd known this was coming; they couldn't move forward with any kind of secrets and distrust between them. She understood that Kit needed to know. If the situations had been reversed and he'd known something about her mum she would have to know too. But this secret was bigger than her and Kit, it could change everything.

She nodded, stroking his face. 'You have to know, I love you. I've fallen in love with you. I know it's only been a few days, but I have never felt this way before about anyone. I know that doesn't change anything, I understand we can't move forward, but you need to know that walking away from you is the hardest thing I'm ever going to do.'

He frowned and then he leaned forward and captured her mouth with his own. She kissed him back, tears falling down her cheeks. How could this be the end when they were so perfect together?

The kiss changed to something more. If this was goodbye, if this was the last time they would be together, then she was damned sure she was going to make the most of it. She slid her hands under his t-shirt, caressing his back, and he groaned against her lips. Clothes were suddenly removed with a frantic, urgent need, his greedy hands exploring her, touching with a desperation she'd not felt from him before. He knew this was goodbye too.

He slipped his hand between her legs and her body instantly responded to his. She moaned against his lips, that feeling exploding through her so hard and fast. He reached over to grab a condom and then he was inside her, gathering her tight against him as if he couldn't bear to let her go. He kissed her hard as she clung to him and she knew with every single fibre of her body that this was where she belonged.

She sensed the shift in her body at the same time she felt his breath catch on her lips and she pulled back to look at him slightly.

'I love you,' she whispered.

He frowned and kissed her, holding her tight as they fell over the edge together.

Zoey was woken in the early hours of the morning as Kit stroked her hair. She was lying on his bare chest.

'Hey, you awake?' he asked. 'We got a hit.'

She sat upright, switching on the bedside lamp. 'Really?'

Kit sat up too and she noticed the phone in his hand. He must have been checking the Google Alerts throughout the night. 'He's trying to sell them.'

'Craig?'

'Well, I don't know for sure, but it's someone in this hotel and it's Craig's level of stupid because look at the photo.'

Kit passed her his phone and she saw the two paintings side by side, propped up on a desk. She couldn't see anything untoward about the photo, but the next photo was of each painting close up and that's when she saw it. On the desk next to the painting was one of the hotel's notepads with 'The Sapphire Bay Hotel' emblazoned across the top.

'Wow, he didn't really think those photos through.'

'No, if it is Craig, he is probably panicking right now. If he tried to check out to coincide with low tide after midnight and was told the police would be stopping cars going over the causeway, I would guess he went straight back to his room and started freaking out over how he could get rid of those paintings before the police came looking for them. He would have taken those photos quickly without thinking about what was in shot. We should go downstairs and see if there's any developments.'

They quickly got dressed and then Kit moved to the door.

'Wait,' Zoey said. 'Hang on a minute. If we actually get these paintings back today then... that's the end of us?'

He stared at her. 'I think that's for the best. My ex-wife was sleeping with someone else almost the entire time we were together and I never knew. I can't start another relationship knowing you have secrets from me too.'

'But this secret doesn't impact on you. This is not me having an affair behind your back, this is something that happened fifteen years ago. It's in the past.'

'But it's my past.'

She felt the lump of emotion burning the back of her throat. 'I'm not ready to say goodbye to you yet. Couldn't we have Christmas together as planned, watch cheesy movies and give each other a present like we talked about, before spending the big day with my mum? Then we go our separate ways.'

He shook his head. 'I don't know, Zoey. I feel like I'm getting in too deep with you and I need to get out before I drown.'

She stared at him. This really was it.

'Come on, let's go get your paintings back,' Kit said.

He opened the door and gestured for her to step outside, which she did, and then he closed the bedroom door behind him.

They walked down the corridor in silence and then down in the lift to the reception. When the doors pinged open, Zoey could see there were police hanging around by the reception desk, talking to the receptionist and Noah and Aria. Other than the police and the hotel staff, there was no one else around, everyone else tucked up in their beds.

Noah waved them over as soon as he saw them. 'Craig tried to check out about an hour ago. When Xena, our receptionist, politely told him that the police were stopping cars at the end of the causeway he seemed to get scared and asked if he could stay another night. Then he returned to his room.'

'Was he carrying the paintings?' Zoey asked.

'Not that I could see,' Xena said. 'But he did have a big suitcase so maybe they were in there.'

'We got a hit on the Google Alerts too,' Kit said. 'He's put a post out trying to sell them. The photos show Sapphire Bay Hotel stationery on the desk.'

'I think we need to go and have a little chat with Mr Ashley,' one of the policemen said.

'Can you search his room without a warrant?' Noah asked. 'I give full permission to go in there if that makes any difference.'

'We don't need a warrant if we're going to arrest him,' the policewoman said. 'Under the Police and Criminal Evidence Act we can arrest him if we have enough reason to suspect he's committed the offence and, once he is under caution, we can then search the room and his belongings. Trying to check out this early in the morning and then changing his mind once he realised we were at the end of the causeway is suspicious enough to give us reasonable grounds to talk to him, but if he refuses to cooperate that would give us reasonable grounds to arrest him.'

Kit's phone beeped in his hand. He glanced at the screen and scowled.

'Is this enough evidence for you? He's just texted my sister to say he has the paintings and will go halves with her if she helps him to get them off the island. She's just forwarded the message to me.'

He passed the phone to the policewoman and she smiled. 'That's pretty much a confession right there. That's definitely enough to make an arrest. Let's go. Mr Campbell, can you show us the way?'

'My pleasure,' Noah said.

Zoey and Kit followed Noah and the police up the stairs to one of the other floors.

The policewoman knocked on the door. 'Mr Ashley, this is the police, can you come to the door?'

Despite the fact that Zoey and Kit were standing well back so as not to get in the way, Zoey distinctly heard Craig give a little squeak of panic. Although he didn't come to the door. He was probably contemplating tying the bed sheets together and trying to escape out of the window.

Noah handed the police the key card and they let themselves in. Zoey could hear a bit of a commotion and then one of the police officers arresting him on suspicion of theft and handling stolen goods before cautioning him.

'You do not need to say anything but it may harm your defence...'

'Wow, that was pretty quick,' Zoey said.

'I just hope he hasn't done anything to damage the paintings,' Kit said.

'It's not fair,' Craig wailed. 'Why does she have them? They were painted by my brother, they should belong to me or his kids.'

After a few moments, the policewoman came out carrying the two paintings in their frames. 'Are these the stolen paintings?'

Zoey nearly sagged in relief at getting them back. 'Yes, these are mine.'

'OK, I'll need to take them out of their frames and photograph them for evidence and you'll have to sign a statement to say that you won't sell them or alter them in any way until after the court case. And you have to agree to produce them for court if required.'

Zoey nodded.

'OK, if you want to wait downstairs in reception, we'll have these back to you shortly. And we'll have to take a statement of your version of events too.'

'OK, thanks.'

Zoey and Kit went downstairs to wait. It wasn't long before a policeman came to take statements from them both and, just as the policewoman had said, Zoey had to sign a form saying she would return the paintings if deemed necessary by the court. And then suddenly it all seemed to be over. The police handed over the paintings and carted Craig off in handcuffs and it was just Kit, Zoey, Noah and Aria left.

'I'm so sorry about all of this,' Aria said. 'This kind of thing doesn't normally happen on Jewel Island and, as you are guests of the hotel and the market, which is organised by the hotel, I do feel this is our responsibility.'

'Please, it wasn't your fault,' Zoey said. 'And we got the paintings back so everything is fine.'

'Even so, I'll give you a voucher to stay in one of our suites for free to apologise for everything you've been through. Now as it's quite late, let me get one of the porters to take you back to your cottage, unless… you're staying here?' Aria said, diplomatically.

Zoey looked at Kit to see if he wanted her to stay but for the first time he looked awkward. He'd already said his goodbyes to her.

Zoey cleared her throat. 'No, a lift back to the cottage would be great.'

Kit nodded.

'Right, I'll just grab one of the porters, I won't be a second,' Aria said, walking off towards the reception desk.

Kit stared at her. 'I'm glad everything worked out OK, with the paintings I mean.'

'Thank you for your help,' Zoey said, quietly.

'I guess I'll probably see you around the market tomorrow. I'm… I'm going to go to one of my friends tomorrow. I'll be closing at lunch so I can get to them for Christmas Eve dinner. I'll be back after Christmas to pack up all my stuff, so I might see you then but if not… take care of yourself, Zoey.'

She watched him turn and go. She had the paintings back but why did it feel like she'd just lost everything?

Kit walked back to his room feeling utterly broken. He should have been happy that they had the paintings back but he couldn't find any happiness right now.

As he rounded the corner before his bedroom, he was surprised to see Sylvia O'Hare standing outside one of the rooms further down the corridor. Dressed in purple satin pyjamas, she still looked as spectacular and glamorous as she did when she was wearing her fancy cloak.

'Are you locked out?' Kit said.

'No, I couldn't sleep and then when I looked out the window and saw all the police cars outside, I thought something exciting might be happening,' Sylvia said.

'Well, art theft and a broken heart,' Kit said. 'I'm not sure I'd call it exciting. But it's all over now, so nothing to see, I'm afraid.'

'Oh no, that doesn't sound good,' Sylvia said. 'Do you want to come in and talk about it?'

Kit smiled, politely. 'With the greatest respect, I'm not about to air my dirty laundry to a woman I barely know.'

'I've been married six times,' Sylvia said. 'I have some experience of the heart.'

Kit sighed. He felt so tired and not just physically, but emotionally too. Maybe it would be good to speak to someone unbiased, someone who could see the relationship from the outside, rather than from his clouded perspective.

'I have a bottle of whisky if that helps sway you.'

'I'm not really a big drinker but I'll come in for one glass,' Kit said.

He followed her back into her room and he watched as

she poured two large glasses of whisky and then passed one to him.

Her large white fluffy dog pulled himself up off the dog bed and came over to sniff Kit. Kit stroked between the dog's ears.

'Tell me everything,' Sylvia said, getting herself comfortable in one of the chairs.

Kit sat down opposite her and the dog settled down next to him so Kit could continue to stroke him. It was somewhat soothing to have the dog there. He carried on stroking the back of the dog's neck and then found himself telling Sylvia everything, about his relationship with Zoey, leaving out any intimate personal details, but including her connection to his dad, all about the paintings, how his uncle had stolen them and how he had now said goodbye to Zoey for good.

Sylvia was quiet for a while, swirling the whisky round in her glass. Kit took a much-needed sip of his, letting the warmth of it fill him from the inside.

'I've had five husbands before my current one. My exes cheated on me, stole from me and one even tried to kill me.'

'What?' Kit said, not expecting that turn of events.

'He threw me overboard on his yacht and left me in the sea to drown. Luckily I was a good swimmer,' Sylvia said, probably glossing over the important details of that moment from her past.

'Christ, I'm sorry, that sounds...' Kit trailed off. He'd had some crappy exes himself but nothing ever that bad.

'It's OK, it was something of a relief in one way. That relationship was a bad one and I was much better out of it.

The point is, I had some awful husbands and I finished with them for very good reasons. I can't imagine ever walking away from the man I loved because of a secret from his past that has no impact on me whatsoever.'

Kit stared down at his glass. Had he made a big mistake? 'Don't you think I have a right to know? This is my dad, not just some random man.'

'Of course you do, but your dad should have told you this as it's quite clearly his secret, not Zoey's. He chose not to tell you and she is trying to be respectful of that. And what if this secret makes you look at your dad in a negative light, surely it's better not knowing that? What difference is knowing that secret going to make after all this time? It will only cause you pain if it's something bad.'

He stroked the dog's velvety ears as he thought.

'What's the worst-case scenario here? What would be the worst thing you could find out about your dad?' Sylvia asked.

'Well, I suppose throwing someone overboard on his yacht would be pretty bad,' Kit said.

Sylvia smiled. 'I didn't know your dad but he didn't strike me as the violent type. Did your dad even have a yacht?'

'No.'

'Then I'm guessing it won't be that.'

'No, I know, a hundred percent that whatever this is, it's not an act of violence. Dad was the gentlest calm man I know. But I suppose the worst thing he could have done would be to have an affair. Him and Mum were always so close and affectionate. To find out that relationship was a lie would make me question everything. I've always said, I wanted what they had, that unbreakable bond. I couldn't stand it if that wasn't true. I suppose the worst thing would be to find out he was having an affair with Zoey's mum. I'm not sure I could move forward with Zoey, knowing that.'

Sylvia sucked in a breath. 'Is there any chance that Zoey could be his daughter too?'

'No, she said that she met Mike when she was nine and he moved in next door to her and her mum.'

'Then I don't see the point in finding out the truth. If you go and bang on her door now and demand to know the truth and she tells you your dad and her mum were at it like rabbits for ten years that's not going to make you feel any better. That will ruin any good memories you have of your dad and, if you do go on to have a relationship with Zoey, then you'll never be able to have any kind of relationship with her mum out of loyalty to your mum. Getting on with your in-laws is an important part of any marriage. I had a ton of crappy in-laws too, trust me when I say you don't want that.'

Kit sighed. He knew she was right. Nothing good would come finding out his dad had a dark and murky past. But he also knew that for the rest of his life he would be wondering what that secret was. Doing his dad a disservice by thinking the worst. He couldn't let this go.

'Real love, the forever kind, is a rare and beautiful thing. It only comes around once in your life, if you're lucky. Some people never find it at all. You said you wanted what your parents had, that unbreakable bond. I wouldn't be so quick to throw that away if I was you.'

'I never said I loved her,' Kit said.

'You didn't have to. I could tell seeing the both of you together, I could tell by the way you talk about her. This is something big and wonderful. You shouldn't be walking away from that.'

Kit sighed and then put his glass down on the side.

'Thanks for the drink.'

He stood up and walked back into his room. He knew Sylvia was right and he didn't want to face the fact he'd probably made the biggest mistake of his life.

CHAPTER 13

CHRISTMAS EVE

Kit's phone rang early the next morning, rousing him from an almost sleepless night. He leaned over to the bedside drawers and answered it.

'Kit, what the hell is going on?' Adam asked by way of a greeting. 'Lindsey has sent me a few vague texts to update me on the way to her holiday. Did Craig really steal those paintings?'

Kit sat up, propping himself up against the headboard ready to fill his brother in.

'Yes. He came here to get money from us, as we suspected. What I didn't see coming was him stealing Dad's paintings from Zoey in order to get that money.'

'Christ, I never thought he'd stoop that low.'

'I know. We got them back though, he made it very easy for the police to connect him to it.'

'That's good. So this woman you've been dating, she has Dad's two lost paintings.'

Kit explained the connection between Zoey and their dad, how he had lived next door to her and taught her how to paint, and how the lost paintings were actually a collaboration between Zoey and their dad.

'Wow, that's a bit of a coincidence that you two met all these years later,' Adam said.

Kit hesitated for a moment. 'There's something else, something she won't tell me, some big secret she is keeping for Dad. I know you said before that if there was something bad about Dad, you wouldn't want to know what it is but I do and I can't let it go. Right now it's coming between us.'

'Christ Kit, I don't envy you in that position.'

'I feel bad because she's trying to protect Dad's secret. I think she feels that Dad chose never to tell us, whatever this thing is, so why should she be the one to break the news now.'

Adam sighed. 'I suppose she has a point. Dad knew he was dying, he had over six months to get his affairs in order, including getting rid of any skeletons from closets, and he never told us some big secret. Maybe it's best if the secret stays buried with him.'

'I feel like I'll always be wondering what it is. What would you do in this situation if Eshana knew something about Dad and refused to tell you?'

Adam was quiet for a moment as he thought. 'I would be annoyed of course, but I love her with everything I have. Nothing is more important than that.'

Kit cursed under his breath. Adam was right. His relationship with Zoey was the most important thing in the world right now. He had to find out whether his dad had an affair, because if the big secret wasn't that then he could probably let this go. Although he wasn't sure what he would do if he found out that was the thing his dad had been keeping from him. But he guessed he would cross that bridge if he came to it.

Kit knocked hard on the door and waited impatiently for an answer. Eventually Beth opened it, immediately looking guilty as soon as she saw him.

'Kit, hello, how lovely to see you,' she said, her voice high with anxiety.

'Zoey told me about those paintings, how she painted the flowers and how she used to paint with my dad, but she wouldn't tell me the rest. She said it wasn't her secret to share, which makes me think it must involve you. So I need to know, were you having an affair with my dad?'

Beth let out a heavy breath. 'Will you come in and we can have a talk about it?'

He hesitated but he knew he needed answers. He nodded and she stepped back to let him inside.

'Can I get you a drink? I was just about to make myself a banoffee hot chocolate.'

'Sure, that sounds nice,' Kit said, marvelling at his ability to keep so calm. His world was falling apart and he was about to sit down and have a hot chocolate with the woman who could be at the heart of it. But he really liked Beth, he couldn't be horrible to her, even if sitting down to hot chocolate with her felt disloyal to his mum.

He followed Beth down to the kitchen and she set about making the hot chocolates.

'I knew you'd think that, what else could you think?' she

said. 'The truth is so implausible that no one would ever even think it, let alone believe it, so you've latched onto the most likely reason Zoey is keeping a secret from you when the reality is far bigger than me and your dad.'

He frowned in confusion.

'Let's address the issue of me and Mike first,' Beth said, placing a mug of hot chocolate in front of him. It smelt sweet and comforting, he hoped it would help.

She sat down opposite him. 'Your dad moved into the flat next to mine a few weeks after I moved into my flat. We'd chat every time we saw each other and we quickly became friends. We just clicked in a way I've never had with anyone before. He was kind and he made me laugh and I'm not ashamed to say I fell in love with him. But I knew nothing was going to happen, he had a wife and children he was utterly in love with. I was happy to just be friends with him. I didn't know anyone in the area and it was lovely to have someone to talk to, even if it was just the weekends. That friendship soon became cooking meals for each other, him spending time helping Zoey to paint, watching movies together. I swear, nothing ever happened, we were just good friends.'

He wanted to believe that, he really did. But even that didn't sound likely. Did nothing really happen between his dad and Beth for ten years when they were clearly so close? A few days before, if Kit had been asked if his dad was loyal and trustworthy, he would have said yes with absolute certainty. He hated that he was now second-guessing everything.

'After his stroke, he was different, cagey. He never

236

painted at home again and he spent more time down in London,' Kit said.

'Yes, there was a reason for that.'

She took a bolstering swig of her hot chocolate before she continued and Kit wasn't sure if he wanted to hear what came next.

'He struggled to paint again after his stroke. You probably know that – his hand just wouldn't do what he wanted it to do. And he'd get so frustrated and upset that he couldn't do the paintings he was famous for, what people expected of him. I'm sure you know that he was so popular that a new Jack Ashley painting was met with almost the same excitement that a new Harry Potter book would receive.'

'It was a lot of pressure for him,' Kit said.

'It was.'

There was a sudden noise at the door and they both looked up to see Zoey standing there staring in horror at them.

'Mum! Have you told him?' Zoey gasped.

'No, but I'm about to,' Beth said.

'You can't.'

'If we don't, Kit will have to live with the fact there is a secret surrounding his dad for the rest of his life. Regardless of what happens between you two, he will always be thinking about it, wondering what it is, his mind making up the worst-case scenarios, like me and Mike having an affair. He needs to know the truth.'

Kit stood up. 'Zoey, I came here today because… because I love you too. I love you so damned much, you have changed my life so completely and the last few days have been the happiest of my life. I'm not willing to throw that away, but I do need to know.'

Zoey stared at him. 'You love me?'

'Yes, and it would destroy Dad to know that this secret is tearing us apart, you know that.'

'We have to tell him,' Beth said. 'We never did anything wrong but he will always assume the worst unless he knows the full story, and Mike deserved better than that.'

Zoey sat down at the table, staring at the cracks in the wood. She didn't speak for the longest time and Kit sat down too, taking her hand. 'Whatever it is, it won't change how I feel for you.'

Zoey let out a hollow laugh. 'I'm pretty sure it will.'

'I'll leave you two alone,' Beth said.

Beth walked out and eventually Zoey nodded. 'OK, I'll tell you.'

Zoey took a deep breath. 'When I first met your dad, I loved his artwork and I used to watch him paint, watch these villages come alive under his hands, and it became something of an obsession. I used to copy his paintings and at first my versions were awful but your dad would patiently teach me about shading and perspective, creating depth with smaller houses to show they were further away. I wanted to learn it all. His paintings were always lying around the house and I would spend hours painstakingly copying each one ten or twenty times over and soon my versions were almost exact copies of his. I was having a hard time at school with a couple of kids bullying me and painting was an escape for me. When I paint it's the only thing I think about: the colours, the textures, bringing little towns to life. I love it.'

She traced a crack across the table with her finger, feeling the sharpness of the rough wood.

'When your dad had his stroke and he couldn't paint any more, I understood that heartache. I could never imagine not being able to paint, but it was worse for him. He had thousands of people round the world waiting for the next Jack Ashley painting, he felt so much pressure and he didn't want to let anyone down or tell anyone that he couldn't do it. His whole life was his art and without that he had nothing. He started to withdraw, you must have seen it. He was depressed, angry. We were losing the man we loved. I had to do something.'

Kit stared at her in horror as the penny finally started to drop.

'So I suggested that I paint for him. My versions were so similar to his, I knew I could recreate his artwork almost exactly as he would have done. So we… collaborated. Only it wasn't just flowers I painted for him now, it was the whole painting. When it was finished he announced to the world he had a new painting and showed off the one I'd painted for him and no one suspected a thing. He was so well-loved that people were just happy to see a new painting, they didn't look that closely. There were those, of course, that spotted the differences but everyone put it down to the fact he'd had a stroke, no one dared criticise the great Jack Ashley. And your dad was happy again, he didn't need to worry about producing the next painting. It was like a huge load had been lifted from his shoulders. Of course that was why he couldn't do the TV show any more, he didn't want people to see him attempting to paint. But he was OK with that. I got the impression that was something of a relief because I don't think he really enjoyed that side of things anyway.'

Kit was looking very pale.

'We thought initially it would be for a few months. He was trying to teach himself to paint with his other hand. But it wasn't just a few months, or a few paintings. He never painted ever again.'

Kit was silent for the longest time and in that moment she knew she had lost him. The way he was staring at her, there wasn't any way back from this.

Kit swallowed. 'There were loads of paintings done after his stroke.'

'Thirty-seven,' Zoey said. 'Thirty-seven of them that had his name on were painted by me.'

Kit's hands were on his face making him look like *The Scream* from Edvard Munch, which was apt considering what they were talking about.

He cleared his throat. 'He was depressed after his stroke, we could see that, and he was spending more and more time in London.'

'Because he didn't want you to see him struggle with his painting – he could barely form a straight line and he was embarrassed by it.'

'He didn't need to be, we were his family. He should have told us the truth. His fans loved him, people would have understood.'

'I think he was worried about letting his family down most of all. You were all so proud of his career as an artist, and he never wanted to admit that that part of his life was over. It felt like admitting defeat and he didn't want to do that.'

He shook his head. 'But... the money that came from his paintings, the sale of the prints...'

'Your dad made sure I was paid. He never got into art for the money, so he didn't really care about that. The mortgage on your family home and his little London flat had been paid off years before, he had money in savings and investments, he was doing fine financially. He wanted to make sure that our arrangement was fair. He put money into an account in my name for every painting I did for him.'

'But... after he died, we sold all those paintings, you should have had some of that money. My mum donated most of it to a stroke charity and then went on a cruise and you—'

'I'm doing fine. And I never did this for the money either, I did it to make your dad happy again. He would have been delighted to see his paintings were helping people who were rebuilding their lives after a stroke or towards important stroke research and I am too.'

Kit played with the tassels on his scarf, focussing on letting them fall between his fingers. 'I can't believe he would go that far to continue his legacy.'

'This kind of thing is far more common than you think. Many artists have a brand that other people contribute towards. And it doesn't just happen in art. Many songs by Robbie Williams were written by Gary Barlow. Ed Sheeran has written songs for One Direction and Justin Bieber. Most of the popular songs in the Top Forty are not written by the person singing it and people are OK with that.'

'But that information on the songwriter is freely available, they don't lie about it.'

'There are lots of books out there supposedly written by some big celebrity when in reality they were written by a ghostwriter. The ghostwriter does all the work, the writing and editing, and gets a flat fee for their contribution from the publisher. People buy the book because of the celebrity name and no one ever knows the truth.'

'What? Is that really what happens?'

Christ, she was ruining all of his beliefs today. She might as well tell him Santa wasn't real and get it over with.

'Sure, not all celebrities obviously. Many celebs write their own books, put in all the hard work, but there are equally as many who have ghostwriters too. This is the same, only, I was a ghost-painter.'

He stood up and went to the window, the snow swirling outside like it was taking part in some crazy dance. 'But… it's lying. The people who buy these stories, these paintings, are doing so because of the name.'

'If people enjoy the paintings or the story, does it really matter if it's done by someone else?'

Kit brushed his hand through his hair. 'People bought paintings believing them to be Jack Ashley art and they weren't. They need to know the truth.'

Anger slammed into Zoey hard. This was precisely the reason she didn't want anyone to know. They would judge and someone decent like Kit would want to do the right thing when actually there was nothing wrong with what she had done. Hundreds of artists had done the same thing for one reason or another over the years. Some were blatant about it, some were more discreet, but it was widely done.

'Hang on a minute, they *were* his paintings, they were his ideas, his inspiration, his style, his direction, his thoughts, his tutelage. It might have been my hands but it was his work.'

He turned to face her.

'I have no regrets about doing what I did, none. Mike was like a father to me, I loved him and after his stroke we were losing the man we loved. He couldn't paint and without that he had no purpose, no outlet to express his creative side. I gave him his life back. I gave him the ability to paint again. And faced with that decision I would do it again in a heartbeat. If you go public with this you ruin the reputation of a wonderful, talented man. All the money that went to charity will be tainted, and for what? We didn't do anything wrong. Those paintings were still his, I just helped him by putting his ideas on paper.'

'I have a video, a few actually, that I took of them painting together,' Beth said, lingering by the doorway. 'It might help to understand the process. Do you want to see?'

Kit nodded keenly, although that was probably in part because seeing any video of his dad would be of interest, no matter what he was doing.

Beth walked in with her laptop and set it up on the table. She pressed play on the clip and Zoey smiled to see Mike sitting next to her at the easel. She must have been around fifteen in this clip; she still had her braces which she'd had off not long after her sixteenth birthday. Her hair was long and not really in any particular style and she looked happy and young and hopeful. Her whole life ahead of her.

'Let's have a house here,' Mike pointed and Zoey pencil-sketched one of the quirky wonky houses that Mike was so famous for. 'And a dog out front in the garden.'

'What kind of dog?'

'A big one, maybe a Great Dane – you like them, don't you?'

'I always wanted one of those. Mum says they're too big.'

'They are too big,' Beth laughed from behind the camera as young Zoey sketched out a large dog with floppy ears.

'OK, let's do the waves now. It's a sunny day so we don't want them too big,' Mike said, pointing with his finger as Zoey recreated his curly styled waves perfectly.

The video came to an end and Zoey looked at Kit, staring at the screen intently.

'Do you want to see another?' Beth said.

Kit nodded.

The next video clip was of Zoey using acrylics to add colour to the piece they had been drawing together in the previous clip.

'Let's mix that turquoise with a bit of white, not too much… that's it,' Mike said. 'OK, just the tips of the waves, that's perfect. And a bit over here too, that's great.'

It made Zoey smile to watch this again. She'd seen it before of course, but it had been several years ago. Painting always had and always would be such a joy for her but nothing compared to those early days of collaborating with Mike on her own paintings initially and then on his. She had loved it and you could visibly see that in the video. You could also see how much pleasure Mike was getting from watching his vision come alive, even if he wasn't the person doing the painting.

'Let's have some of that viridian on the trees over here... No wait, that's too dark, add a bit of yellow.'

Zoey smiled as she watched herself squeeze a tiny bit of yellow onto her palette and then use her fingers to smear the green and the yellow together on the paper.

'That's a great colour, but just do this part of the tree, the rest of it can stay dark,' Mike said. 'And let's do the next tree the same.'

She chanced a look at Kit, who wasn't saying a word, just staring at the screen. He looked so serious, so... emotional. It must be so hard to take all this in.

'Right, we need some shading here on the side of this building, let's have a bit of burnt umber mixed with some sangria,' Mike was saying, but Zoey leaned forward and pressed pause on the clip.

'I think perhaps that we should forward these clips to Kit so he can watch them in his own time. If you leave us your email, we can send them over,' Zoey said gently.

He nodded and grabbed a piece of paper and a pen and quickly scrawled down his email address. 'I need to go. Thanks for the hot chocolate. And your honesty.'

He wrapped his scarf around him.

'Kit, I'm sorry if this wasn't what you wanted to hear and I know you must be feeling hurt that your dad didn't tell you the truth. I understand that all of this might make it difficult for us to be together,' she swallowed the lump of emotion in her throat. 'But if you want to talk about any of this, ask any questions about your dad, then I'm always here, regardless of what happens between us.'

He nodded.

'And please, before you do anything hasty, before you do something you can never take back, please come and talk to me first.'

She hated the thought that telling Kit could ruin Mike's reputation after all this time. He was a wonderful man and he didn't deserve that.

Kit nodded again and then walked out onto the street, the snow whipping around him.

Zoey closed her hut for the last time and looked at the sky as the snow came down thick and fast. A white Christmas was definitely looking like a possibility. As a big fan of Christmas this should have filled her with joy but she felt empty inside. She'd been by Kit's hut several times throughout the day but it had been resolutely closed, and she wondered if he had already packed up and left to have Christmas with his friends and whether she'd ever see him again. The thought of that hurt, especially as he had said he loved her. How could he really let this thing come between them?

She turned to Marika, who was locking up her hut too. 'Are you off to your parents tonight?'

'Yes, they aren't far from here. I'll be with them for the big day and then Elias has said he'll come and stay with me on the twenty-sixth for a few days. It'll be nice to get to know each other outside of the market, take our time.'

Zoey smiled. There had been no taking her time with Kit, she had fallen fast and hard, which was silly really. She should have learned from her mistake with David and taken a more cautious approach when embarking on a new relationship.

Marika grinned at her as if reading her thoughts. 'You and Kit have something special. Sometimes you should hold back, go slow, and sometimes you meet someone wonderful and you should embrace that and throw caution to the wind, enjoy the magic, even if that time is fleeting.'

'I think our time has come and gone,' Zoey said. She hadn't told Marika about her connection to Kit's dad or the paintings, just that she and Kit had come to an impasse and there didn't look like there was any way past that.

'From what I saw, you two looked like you'd found forever. Whatever this is, I'm sure you'll find a way.'

'I hope so.'

'Are you at your mum's tonight?' Marika asked.

Zoey shook her head. 'She's gone out for Christmas drinks with her knitting group, but I'll be with her all day tomorrow.'

'Well, I'll probably see you around after all the festivities, I'll be back to clear out my hut,' Marika said.

'And you can always come and visit me here in my new home next year, whenever you come down to see your parents. It'd be good to keep in touch.'

'I'd like that.'

'Have a good Christmas, I hope it's filled with piparkakut, joulutorttu and glögi,' Zoey said, hoping she'd got the pronunciation right.

Marika laughed. 'Thank you. Merry Christmas, Zoey.'

Zoey gave her a hug and then watched as Marika walked off into the snow as if the cold wind and whirling flakes didn't bother her at all.

Zoey tugged her scarf tighter around her neck, pulled her hood up and made the short journey back to her cottage.

She felt so disappointed that her relationship with Kit had gone so badly wrong. She understood, when she'd kept the secret from him that he was upset with that, it wasn't just a secret about her own life, it was a secret about his dad. But now she'd come clean, what was holding him back?

He didn't understand that what she'd done for his dad was a necessity. The paintings were still his. She didn't see it as cheating or lying and she felt hurt that Kit did.

She moved around the lake, remembering that first night he'd stripped off to rescue a rabbit. She'd known then that he was something special and not just because he'd been prepared to risk his life to save the animal but because of the way they'd clicked so well. She'd had so much hope for them and now it was all over.

Zoey approached her house and stopped dead because, huddled against the doorway, was a shadowy figure. She couldn't see his face but she knew instantly it was Kit.

She found herself running the last few metres to her door. 'What are you doing here?'

'I came to talk to you.'

He looked absolutely frozen as she quickly fumbled with the key to open the door. 'How long have you been here?'

'A while. I didn't want to leave and end up missing you.

I figured you might close early as it's Christmas Eve. It seems I was wrong.'

'Christ, you could have just come and seen me at the hut.' Zoey opened the door and bundled him inside. She quickly lit the fire and then turned back to face him. He was still hunched inside his coat. 'Sit in front of the fire. I'll make you a hot chocolate.'

'No, wait, we need to talk.'

'No, we need to get you warm first. You can't talk to me if you die from hypothermia. Now sit down.'

He did what he was told, kneeling down in front of the log burner, and she rushed off to the kitchen.

She took a few minutes to make the drinks, her racing heart changing from worry to anticipation. What was he doing here?

She rushed back into the lounge and saw he was sitting on the floor, his feet and hands outstretched towards the fire.

She passed him the hot chocolate and then grabbed a blanket from the back of the sofa and wrapped it around him as she knelt down next to him.

Kit turned to face her. 'God, you're so lovely.' He cupped her face with one hand, trailing his thumb over her cheek and lips. 'And I don't deserve it.'

She smiled. 'You definitely deserve it. Whatever happens between me and you, you're still one of the loveliest men I've ever met.'

He stared at her, his eyes scanning across her face, taking her in. 'We need to talk.'

He was obviously here to talk more about his dad.

'I'm sorry that you had to find out the truth like that but I truly don't believe we were doing anything wrong.'

'I watched the videos, probably a hundred times. And I don't either. God he looked so happy, like he always used to do when he was painting. I'm sad that because of the stroke he lost that but you gave it back to him. You weren't just drawing houses, you were painting *his* style of houses, *his* style of people and animals and under his instruction. You're right, they were *his* paintings, his designs and ideas, even down to what colours you should use and where. And I had no right to get high and mighty and judgemental about any of it. You saved his life, and not just immediately after the stroke when you called the ambulance, but after, when he'd become so withdrawn and upset about not being able to paint any more. You saved him then too and I will always be grateful for that. We were losing him and you gave him back to us.'

'I loved him too and I hated watching him fade away. I had to do something.'

'You definitely did the right thing.'

'So you're not going to go public with this?'

'He had some help with his paintings. Is it really any different to an author getting help from an editor, or a pop star getting help with his songs? It was still his brand, his style. The people who bought his art still got a Jack Ashley painting. I have no doubt about that. But actually they got something better than that. They bought a brilliant collaboration that was born out of passion for art and to continue my dad's legacy. There is so much of you in those paintings, your love and loyalty for my dad shine through every brush stroke and I never want to do anything to ruin that.'

Zoey let out a breath of relief.

'But I didn't come here to talk about my dad, not really. I came here because I love you and none of what's happened in the last few days with the paintings, with the secret, has changed that. In fact, it's made me love you even more.'

Her heart was thundering against her chest as she stared at him.

'You are... magnificent. You're the most amazing woman I've ever met. What you did for my dad is a small part of it, but what you've done for me is so much more. You've changed my world completely and I know it's still early days for us but this feels like it could be forever. I love—'

Kit's words were lost as she leaned forward and kissed him hard. He fell back onto the carpet with her on top of him and he laughed against her lips.

'I love you too,' Zoey said, wrestling him out of his clothes and he helped her out of hers. 'But don't get any ideas. When people get really cold, body heat is important to keep them warm.'

He rolled on top of her, kissing her throat. 'Body heat is a great idea.'

Zoey woke wrapped in Kit's arms as they lay in her bed. Outside, snow was gently falling, making the world seem a brighter, happier place.

She leaned up to look at the man she loved. 'Well, last night didn't go according to plan.'

He stroked her hair. 'What do you mean?'

'I thought we were going to start all these Christmas Eve traditions, watch movies, have a proper three-course meal, roast marshmallows on the fire. Give each other a present, stay up until midnight and toast Christmas with a glass of champagne, I had it all planned.'

'Well that sounds lovely.'

'But instead we made love in every room of the house, ate a ton of churros, had more sex and passed out from exhaustion around eleven.'

Kit grinned. 'I have to say, that was my best Christmas Eve ever, I think we should do that every year.'

Zoey smiled. 'It was pretty special.'

'We can do those things tomorrow night, make the Christmas celebrations last even longer.'

'That sounds good. So you're a fan of Christmas now?'

'The last few days, I have cut my hand on the wire we were using to make wreaths, cut my chin when I was ice skating and been given a poo ornament to hang on our tree. But right now, Christmas is definitely my favourite time of the year, but especially when it starts like this, lying in bed with the woman I love.'

'I think every day from now on will start like this,' Zoey said.

'I hope so. In all seriousness, you have given me back my love of Christmas again, and not just because I spent Christmas Eve having amazing sex. You have showed me what this season is truly about. Fun, happiness and making memories with the people you love.'

She grinned.

'And I do love you Zoey Flynn,' Kit said.

She leaned up and kissed him.

'I know you wanted to take the time to get this right,' Kit said. 'And I do too. I've already spoken to Aria and this cottage is free for the whole of January. I thought I would stay here, help you settle into your cottage overlooking the harbour, and if we are still going strong after that...'

'You could move in with me,' Zoey said, knowing even as she said it that nothing would feel more right than them sharing a house together. She could imagine them both in that cottage so clearly. Their happy ever after.

He smiled. 'If that's what you want, but I'm happy to take this as slow as you want to.'

'Marika said to me that sometimes you meet someone

and you should hold back, take things slow, and sometimes you meet someone and you should go with the flow. She said we have that forever kind of love and we should definitely embrace that. I think it's a great idea you staying here while we get to know each other better, but, after that, it'll be time for you to come home.'

He nodded and kissed her again. She could definitely get used to waking up like this.

'And it has quite a large garden,' Kit said, pulling back slightly. 'So maybe we can get that Great Dane too.'

'Oh my god, I would love that,' Zoey said. 'But what about the donkey?'

Kit laughed. 'We can put a pin in the donkey for now.'

'Nix owns a bit of land on the other side of the island, maybe he might rent out a small part of it.'

'Now that's an idea.'

'Right, shall we do presents?' Zoey said, excitedly.

'OK, I have yours here,' Kit said, climbing out of bed and grabbing his jeans. He fished out a small black box and handed it to her.

Her heart leapt. While she had every confidence that what she had with Kit was forever, a marriage proposal so soon was a tiny bit surprising, especially after his speech about taking things slow.

He chuckled. 'Your face. It's not that, I promise.'

She laughed in relief. She opened it up and inside was a necklace with a glass droplet. But inside was what appeared to be a snowflake.

'It's a real snowflake, perfectly preserved forever inside a special polymer. You said you always wanted to keep the snow when you were a child, well now you can.'

She stared at it. 'Kit, this is beautiful. Thank you.'

'Here, let me put it on,' he said.

She swivelled to face away from him and he wrapped the necklace around her neck, his touch sending wonderful goosebumps across her body. She held it up to the light and smiled to see the fractures of tiny rainbows dancing off the snowflake.

'I love it, thank you. I have one for you that I can't wait to show you. This was going to be your Christmas Eve present. I have a few other little things you can open when we get to Mum's but you can open this now.'

She quickly scrambled out of bed and ran downstairs, grabbing the picture she had been working on for the last few days. She went back upstairs and climbed back into bed, handing it over.

'Thank you,' Kit said, tearing away the tissue paper she'd wrapped it in. He stared at it, his eyes scanning over the details. At first glance he would see a little village scene of Jewel Island, the shops, the sea, even the little Christmas market in one corner. But if he looked closer he could see the little couples she'd added at various points in the village. The man throwing a bucket of water over the woman in the bottom of the scene, sitting on the beach eating fish and chips in the mouth of the cave, the half-naked man crawling on the lake in the top of the picture to save a rabbit. There was a couple in the middle decorating a tree and another couple sitting at a stand in the Christmas market icing cookies. In fact every single couple in the picture was depicting the various things that had happened in their relationship so far.

'Oh my god, this is amazing,' Kit said.

'It's the story of us,' Zoey said. 'Only it's not quite finished. Maybe over here we can have a couple coming out of their house overlooking the harbour and then a couple walking their Great Dane on the beach.'

'I love that idea,' Kit said. 'Maybe one day we can add a bride and groom coming out of the church over here and then a pregnant couple over here, with the woman wearing a Christmas pudding jumper.'

Her heart leapt. 'I'd love that.'

He stared at her. 'I'm going to ask you to marry me one day.'

'And I will say yes.'

He grinned and leaned forward to kiss her.

Kit couldn't help smiling about how his Christmas Day had turned out. He had arrived on Jewel Island with no expectations that he'd have any kind of Christmas celebration at all, still feeling sore over how his last Christmas had gone. He'd been considering going to a friend's house for Christmas Day but would have been more than happy sitting in his hotel room, ordering room service and watching trashy TV to pass the big day itself.

And now he was sitting here in Beth's lounge, the log fire burning happily in the fireplace, a glass of mulled wine in his hand, Zoey cuddled up by his side as they watched Beth desperately try to win at Pictionary as she tried to convey something on her piece of paper. He hadn't laughed this much in a long time.

They'd eaten until they were well and truly stuffed,

they'd shared presents, with Zoey disguising a Toblerone for him wrapped in a ton of bubble wrap, they'd watched cheesy movies and played games for most of the afternoon. It couldn't have been more perfect.

They'd talked about his dad too, the anecdotes that Kit had of his dad cremating the turkey, or the stories Zoey and her mum had of Mike helping them to ice the Christmas cake, very badly. It was wonderful to hear all these new memories he'd never heard before.

Although he had to admit, as lovely as the day had been, it had only been so perfect because he got to spend it with the woman he loved with his entire heart. He had never before been so convinced of his future. Even when he'd been engaged to Lily, when he'd been blissfully unaware of the secrets and lies, there had been niggles, things that just didn't feel right. With Zoey, he knew he was going to grow old and grey with this wonderful woman by his side.

She giggled against him as Beth continued to point frantically to her picture. He'd quickly realised that Beth's method to Pictionary was to spend a few seconds drawing and the rest of her time pointing to different parts of the picture. Beth's talent clearly didn't lie in drawing. She was gesturing to something on the top of her drawing which possibly could be a star. With three seconds to spare, Kit suddenly realised what it was.

'Is it a Christmas tree?'

Beth nearly collapsed in her chair in relief. 'Yes, of course it is.'

Zoey snorted into his shoulder before getting up and stretching. 'I think we might head back to my cottage. The snow is still coming down and we don't want to get snowed in.'

'Good idea,' Kit said. Although he had ideas of his own of how to finish celebrating Christmas Day with Zoey, even if there wasn't much of the big day left.

'Come round for lunch tomorrow, there's tons of left-over turkey to get through,' Beth said, following them to the door.

'We'd be happy to,' Kit said.

They bundled themselves into coats and scarves and with lots of hugs all round they stepped out into the street.

The snow was gentler now than it had been a few hours before, fluttering to the ground under the glow of the Christmas lights. The streets were empty as they left snowy footprints behind them and made their way back up to the hotel and Moonstone Cottage.

'Thank you for a wonderful Christmas,' Kit said.

'Oh, it's been lovely,' Zoey said. 'I've had the most magical day.'

They walked round the lake towards her cottage. Thankfully there were no rabbits that needed rescuing this time.

They approached the cottage door.

'Oh look, mistletoe,' Zoey said innocently, pointing to a small sprig of white berries hanging above them.

He grinned. 'So there is.'

Suddenly the church clock in the village started ringing out for midnight.

'We should make a Christmas wish,' Kit said.

'Oh yes,' Zoey said excitedly and he smiled when she

scrunched up her eyes. God he loved her; she filled his heart to the very top.

As the last gong rang out, he bent his head and kissed her. She started in surprise for a second before wrapping her arms round his neck and kissing him back.

He pulled away slightly to look at her. 'What did you wish for?'

'Forever with you,' Zoey said. 'What did you wish for?'

'That whatever you wished for came true.'

She grinned and kissed him again.

He slid his arms around her, holding her close, and he knew he would always remember this moment when their wishes came true. This was the start of their forever, standing under the mistletoe at Moonstone Lake.

STAY IN TOUCH...

To keep up to date with the latest news on my releases, just go to the link below to sign up for a newsletter. You'll also get two FREE short stories, get sneak peeks, booky news and be able to take part in exclusive giveaways. Your email will never be shared with anyone else and you can unsubscribe at any time

https://www.subscribepage.com/hollymartinsignup

Website: https://hollymartin-author.com/
Email: holly@hollymartin-author.com
Twitter: @HollyMAuthor

Jewel Island Series

Sunrise over Sapphire Bay

Autumn Skies over Ruby Falls

Ice Creams at Emerald Cove

Sunlight over Crystal Sands

Mistletoe at Moonstone Lake

The Happiness Series

The Little Village of Happiness

The Gift of Happiness

The Summer of Chasing Dreams

The Secrets of Clover Castle

(Previously published as Fairytale Beginnings)

Sandcastle Bay Series

The Holiday Cottage by the Sea

The Cottage on Sunshine Beach

Coming Home to Maple Cottage

Hope Island Series
Spring at Blueberry Bay
Summer at Buttercup Beach
Christmas at Mistletoe Cove

Juniper Island Series
Christmas Under a Cranberry Sky
A Town Called Christmas

White Cliff Bay Series
Christmas at Lilac Cottage
Snowflakes on Silver Cove
Summer at Rose Island

Standalone Stories
Tied Up With Love
A Home on Bramble Hill
One Hundred Christmas Proposals
One Hundred Proposals

The Guestbook at Willow Cottage

For Young Adults

The Sentinel Series

The Sentinel (Book 1 of the Sentinel Series)

The Prophecies (Book 2 of the Sentinel Series)

The Revenge (Book 3 of the Sentinel Series)

The Reckoning (Book 4 of the Sentinel Series)

A LETTER FROM HOLLY

Thank you so much for reading *Mistletoe at Moonstone Lake,* I had so much fun creating this story and including all the Christmas magic. I hope you enjoyed reading it as much as I enjoyed writing it.

One of the best parts of writing comes from seeing the reaction from readers. Did it make you smile or laugh, did it make you cry, hopefully happy tears? Did you fall in love with Kit and Zoey as much as I did? Did you like the little Christmas market on Jewel Island? If you enjoyed the story, I would absolutely love it if you could leave a short review on Amazon. Getting feedback from readers is amazing and it also helps to persuade other readers to pick up one of my books for the first time.

Thank you for reading.

Love Holly x

ACKNOWLEDGEMENTS

To my family, my mom, my biggest fan, who reads every word I've written a hundred times over and loves it every single time, my dad, my brother Lee and my sister-in-law Julie, for your support, love, encouragement and endless excitement for my stories.

For my twinnie, the gorgeous Aven Ellis for just being my wonderful friend, for your endless support, for cheering me on, for reading my stories and telling me what works and what doesn't and for keeping me entertained with wonderful stories. I love you dearly.

To my lovely friends Julie, Natalie, Jac, Verity and Jodie, thanks for all the support.

To the Devon contingent, Paw and Order, Belinda, Lisa, Phil, Bodie, Kodi and Skipper. Thanks for keeping me entertained and always being there.

To everyone at Bookcamp, you gorgeous, fabulous bunch, thank you for your wonderful support on this venture.

Thanks to the brilliant Emma Rogers for the gorgeous cover design.

Thanks to my fabulous editors, Celine Kelly and Rhian McKay.

Huge thanks to the lovely Graham Bartlett, former detective, brilliant crime writer and a crime fiction and police advisor who gave me some great advice on the police scenes and what they would legally be allowed to do.

To all the wonderful bloggers for your tweets, retweets, facebook posts, tireless promotions, support, encouragement and endless enthusiasm. You guys are amazing and I couldn't do this journey without you.

To anyone who has read my book and taken the time to tell me you've enjoyed it or wrote a review, thank you so much.

Thank you, I love you all.

978-1-913616-29-8 Paperback
978-1-913616-30-4 Large Print paperback
978-1-913616-31-1 Hardback

Cover design by Emma Rogers

Printed in Great Britain
by Amazon